DEAR AUGUSTUS

I

Never

Let

Go

DEAR AUGUSTUS
I Never Let Go

POOJA PATHAK

Published by
Author's Ink Publications
Info@authorsinkindia.com
authorsinkindia@gmail.com
Facebook: www.facebook.com/authorsinkindia
Twitter: www.twitter.com/authorsinkindia
Our Blog: authorsinkindia.com/blog
Contact: +91-8950970646

ISBN: xxxx

Typeset by Nikhil Mahajan in 11 pts Garamond.
Printed and bound in India.

To those who know what it feels like to be a warrior in a lost battle. Quitting is not an option. You fight till the end.

"In the end we discover that to love and let go can
be the same thing."

— Jack Kornfield

He was like a song of forever glee, the one I'd wished for often.

As bright as the sunshine and free-spirited as showers of rain.

A love I craved to hold but had to let go of anyway.

Every single time.

Again, and again and again.

_____

Tell me we are in it

together

day and night

for as long as we live,

and I will wait for you

in the abyss

forever.

_____

00 | Dear Augustus

And some days, you feel so empty that you fill the voids with thoughts that eventually make you feel more shattered. But you'd still rather do that than not feel anything at all. And some days, you feel so lost that you stray into the memories of those good old days instead of being nowhere at all.

On the way to the airport two years ago, my heart was empty. I wanted to run back to you and stop you from letting me go or beg you to make me stay even for a few more seconds, but I didn't. Ugly tears of pain and heartbreak pelted down my eyes along with the black strokes of mascara I had so thoughtlessly applied that morning.

As soon as I walked out of the old housing estate, my legs turned shaky with the impact of pain in my chest, and my throat felt itchy with the restraint to look back, knowing you were watching me leave from the window ledge.

I was drowning, breaking, falling with each step I took away from you. Whoever said young love is the easiest to forget has never truly experienced it, I'm sure. Because it damn near felt like dying. My knees almost gave up as I walked out of the rusty old doors and wrapped my arms around me to escape the evening breeze. A flash of lightning rumbled across the gray sky above me, blowing me up a bit.

The spell broke, and I took the last chance to look back at the window. We had spent many evenings lost in the strings of your music and my heart. The window was shut, as were you.

"Goodbye, Violet," you'd whispered while I shook my head frantically.

As the moment replayed in my mind, I no longer controlled my tears and let them succumb to my woe.

"Go, and do not turn back."

I never wanted anything as intensely as to erase the echo of those words from my memory.

Poor Violet, you fall in love instinctively, not knowing when to pull yourself out of it.

Just as my knees were about to hit the ground, his protective arms wrapped around me, shielding me from the blistering winds of loss and hurt. And for the second time that day, I wished those arms were yours. Adrian placed a soft kiss on the back of my head, pulling me away from the heartache, and then I was in the car, reeling away from the town.

I buried my face against his chest as he rubbed soothing circles on my back. Words of hope, assurance and a promise of a new world reverberated from his lips as I wept for a love that cut ever deeper. The scent of familiarity mixed with the smell of clean linen engulfed me as he pushed away a tear-stained hair from my face.

"Does love always hurt this much?" I croaked out. "Have you ever felt like this, Adri?"

Adrian released a strangled sigh, looking down at me. "I'm yet to experience it, but when I do, I hope we get over it together."

The love I experienced was venomous. It took away every sweet thing I wrote about love in my poems, then left me with bitterness in the dark. I would never wish the same for Adrian or anyone else.

Adrian's calm heartbeat vibrated against my ear as he held me through my pain, and I eventually drifted off to sleep.

"Goodbye, Violet. Go and do not turn back."

Those were the last words when you let me go, and they would always be a reminder of the perfect self-ruination.

-Violet

01 | Let Your Heart Heal

As hard as it may seem, some pain needs to be buried overnight, forcing your heart to toughen up for tomorrow. So you do not miss the opportunity to move on and do not feel vulnerable in the hands of those who can only cause more pain to your soul.

Falling in love is simple. Letting go of the same is not so. It is to say goodbye to the very feeling that pushed you towards a welcoming hello. And somehow, it feels like falling in love all over again. Only the intensity is much stronger. You try sleeping it off or crying a river of what-ifs, but no amount of tossing and turning in your bed can erase the memories.

The storm only gets fiercer with time as your dimpled smile, the fiery brushes of your fingertips, and the sweet melody of your deep voice are the only dreams that inhabit my sleep.

Letting you go is the most unaccomplished task of my life, but I wonder if it is the only way to heal.

***

There are days of pure bliss when I don't need to listen to any motivational podcast and further drain my mind into believing it's not in peace. The dull ache of losing a vital part of my growth is always there, like when my friends talk about their prospective dates or love interests, and I get dragged to my good old high school days when I was as miserable in my love life as I am now. These are the worst days of my life.

On such days I keep myself busy with university assignments or my work at the cafe. Both are an integral part of my life. My academics will lead me to my dream job, and the work at the coffee house will keep my bank account from drying out.

Work is always a great distraction from the unsettled thoughts that keep plunging me ten feet deeper into the ocean of my memories. Thoughts, my mind is always buzzing with them at odd times like now as I look up intently into his amber eyes. It's been a long time. But every time someone with eyes of pure resemblance to yours comes into view, my head explodes with images of the most beautiful but painful moments of my life.

Maybe I'm just homesick, but going back to the town makes it worse. In the last three years, a lot has changed in *Winsbay*, including the fact that it's missing you too, dear Augustus. No one knows where you went, not that I wish to know. But on a few lonely nights, I dream about visiting home on my mini cooper and bumping into you. The dream ends on your charming face with a dimpled smile and golden hair, an unwelcome pain seeping through the cracks of my heart.

These dreams are becoming less frequent but haven't stopped altogether.

Days like today are somewhat bearable as I sit at one of the empty tables in the cafeteria, trying to solve some calculus. It's never going to be easy for me. No matter how much I practice, there's always a chance of me messing it up during the exams. Half-eaten sandwich, begging to finish in the last 20 minutes, but I've been stuck with this integral since this morning. As I keep tapping my pen on the unsolved problem, occasionally groaning out curses at myself for choosing mathematics over literature, my moment is interrupted by one of the guys from the soccer team.

I pause and look up to collide with his amber eyes, the same texture, no difference, not a single tone. This charming boy- I have seen many times before but never up close, never close enough to notice the exact color of his eyes. It can't be a good thing because now, as I look into his eyes, all the band-aids I had applied over the years are ripped open.

"Are you coming to the party at my place tomorrow night?" Liam repeats, breaking my train of thought. They resurface due to the painful similarities he exhibits to someone I can never get rid of in my mind. He shifts restlessly, leaning against my table and running his well-defined hands through his messy brown hair.

Not golden like yours.

As he pulls out the empty chair beside me, I notice the sheen of sweat covering his forehead and the sharp edges of his cheekbones. His sports jersey sticks to his noticeably defined body, and the running shorts admit his arrival straight from the game. He doesn't give me enough breath to reply and drops his soccer bag to the floor as he settles down.

I try to give him my full attention, but I can feel a set of fiery green eyes boring the side of my face. I don't need to turn at the source to tell whose eyes are those. The entire soccer team has arrived at the cafeteria, and along with them is their captain, Adrian Hayes. While others grin at Liam's bold move toward me, Adrian glares.

I let my gaze stay locked on those amber eyes. The moment a sly grin appears on Liam's face, my daze breaks. He sips the water from the disposable bottle in his right hand and stares at me for a response. His confident eyes give me a quick once-over before they settle on my face.

It's been so long since anyone has invited me to their private parties. The ones my roommate hosts at our place are the only exceptions. On those occasions, the usual crowd is people I can hardly interact with or form any connection with. The soccer guys never look my way because of their captain. But that changes today. Adrian can't decide who is good for me and who is not. Even more, when he has hardly spoken two words since our sophomore year.

Just say yes this once.

"Okay." A single word is all I can make of looking at his face. I fail to avoid the chills erupting at the back of my neck due to the stare Adrian gives me. A shrill scraping sound rings through the room as he pulls back the empty chair across me and settles, looking straight at my heated face. I keep my poker face on and give a half-assed smile to the charming boy beside me.

"Here, can you punch in your number?" He hands me his cell phone and watches me tapping his fingers on the table as I save my number on his phone.

"Cool," Liam says with a wink, getting up almost as fast as he settled. "I promise. You won't regret it. My place tomorrow, then. I will be waiting for you, V."

I hear a loud thud as Adrian places the smoothie in his hand on the table. His knuckles are red due to the pressure with which he is holding the glass. I can never get his deal. One moment he avoids my existence, and another moment he behaves all possessively about me. It wasn't always like this, and I'm confused about this change.

"See you at the party," I arrange my mouth in a smile and glance at the scowling boy across from me.

Liam secures his bag over his shoulder and walks backward with his hands in his jeans pockets. "I'm happy to have your attention, finally. It took me three years, but I'm not stepping back."

"He wants to get in your pants." Adrian clips sharply as soon as Liam and the guys exit the cafeteria. I wonder why Adrian is still here. More importantly, his words ignite a dormant rage that I have been hiding for almost a year.

"And you are getting on my nerves." I shift uncomfortably and pin him with a scoff. I notice the slight shift in his jaw as he clenches his teeth and gulps down his anger. I don't know what made him so worked up. I have to admit the charms that radiate through the boy sitting across from me are hard to brush off.

Over the years, he has grown so much and is nothing less than a character straight from romance novels, the type you swoon over. Girls from all years fancy him since he set foot in college, and he never even has to work to get their attention. But then that tends to happen everywhere he goes. He has the body of an athlete, a chiseled jawline, and sea-green eyes, which are too difficult to ignore. For me, though, he is still the boy I have known all my life.

"Every set of amber eyes doesn't belong to your goldilocks," Adrian grits, running his hand aggressively through his tousled dark brown hair. "Also, next time someone calls you V, I'm ripping their tongue out. I mean it. No one calls you V except me."

Okay, that's enough.

"What's your deal Adri?" I release a shocked laugh. "If someone likes to call me V, they will. It should not concern you."

"Don't do something stupid that's all I wanted to tell you. You can choose anyone to date or rebound but be thoughtful about who you choose. Liam is not prey. He is a predator. And you sure as hell won't be his prey. Not on my watch." His scowl deepens, and I gulp at the sparks that zip up my spine. It's a new feeling, and his constant eye contact isn't helping.

"Stop behaving like my brother," I snap, clenching my fingers tightly underneath the table.

He walks out of his seat at lightning speed and stands behind me. Suddenly, the proximity is a thing as he breathes against my ear. The heat of his body transfers to mine. "After what happened last year, don't you think calling me your brother is a bit inappropriate?"

His words leave me speechless. A silent tremor erupts in my belly as I remember the incident he is talking about, and I can't help the blush that creeps up my cheeks. Oh God, he still remembers it. Not that I have forgotten, but the memory only confuses me further.

"Drink it," he says in a thick voice, placing the glass of blueberry smoothie beside my half-eaten sandwich. The last time I drank a smoothie was with you, Augustus. But somehow, for the first time in years, I want to drink this one.

"And for fucks sake, be a little careful with Liam. I mean it, V." He steps away, and when I gather myself to turn back, he is already out of the cafeteria.

My heart is a mess with a tangled past and a twisted new fate.

02 | A Taste of Familiarity

One year ago

I watched Adrian from the bleachers as he did laps around the field. He was running when I arrived there, and I knew it wasn't for the upcoming soccer game. It was way too aggressive to count it as a warm-up. I could tell he was pissed and blowing off steam.

When he texted me in the afternoon about an impromptu lunch with his father, I knew where to find him after the epic reunion. It was late in the evening, and from where I sat, it was just the two of us. So, he had no reason to ignore my presence and behave closed off. He hated talking about his father's new married life, but no one knew better than me how toxic concealing your feelings could be.

I unzipped my sweatshirt and peeled it off my body to leave myself in my running shorts, sports bra, and tank top. I tied the shoelaces of my Nikes, giving another look at the angry bull chasing after the red blaring inside his head. He knew why I had decided to join him for the run that evening, and it wasn't just to make sure he didn't fall back to his old addiction. He had grown out of doing that teenage stuff. It was to be there for him even when he wouldn't allow anyone.

His father was always a sour spot for him, and the more he tried to dodge his advances to make things better between them, the more it hurt him. That explained his crazy marathon around the soccer field.

I grabbed my phone, stuck the earbuds in my ears, and put on my running playlist, all the upbeat Indie pop numbers I could rely on if he continued his silent treatment. I took a deep breath, inhaling the cool evening breeze, stretching briefly, and then tightened my ponytail before taking off, joining the sweaty athlete.

I started in the opposite direction and almost bumped into Adrian. He halted just before the impact and huffed out. I cursed myself mentally for blocking the path of an angry bull. He was breathing heavily, waiting for me to either step aside from his way or say something, but I couldn't process the view in front of me.

He was sweating heavily. His shoulders were tense, and he was shirtless in gym shorts that hugged his toned thighs perfectly. I'd seen him practicing like that since we were kids, but it felt like I'd been seeing someone else all this time. His sculpted abs rippling down his toned torso, a dark line of hair running down his stomach that disappeared beneath his shorts, had me fanning for all the fire he set around me. I gulped down a butterfly stuck in my throat. He ran a hand through his messy brown hair and flexed his broad shoulders while placing his hands on his hips. Directing a scowl at me, he wiped away the lines of sweat from his forehead and raised his brow in question.

No way I was getting hot and flustered by looking at Adrian. I had a crush on him since I was fourteen, but that changed when I met you. Yes, you, Augustus. I should be thinking about you, not my best friend. I clenched my fists tightly at my sides, nails digging into my palms to snap out of whatever fuzzy feelings, his sea-green eyes instilled in me. He cracked his neck with a quick tilt making me swallow hard, and resumed running. The way he stepped away from my path showed he could look right through my emotions and knew I was thinking about him.

I pushed away all the tension that surrounded us at that moment and fell into step next to him. He let our footsteps sync for a few seconds before picking the pace, which I matched, then we increased our speed, and we ran around the field, syncing our steps, breathing hard and sweating. We didn't speak or even look at each other until his pace became too much to match, and I somehow lost my footing, twisting my ankle in the process. I landed too hard, jarring my ankle to the point that a cry of pain escaped my mouth as I fell forward.

"V!" Adrian's panicked voice reached my ear as the earbuds flew off along with me. But before I could hit the ground, Adrian caught me. His arms came around me and his green eyes filled with worry never left my face as he hooked one of his arms beneath my knees, the other one around my shoulders, and then, he was carrying me.

For a moment, my mind malfunctioned due to the comfort I felt nestled up in his strong arms. It was wrong on so many levels. First, he felt too familiar, too natural, and too comforting. Second, a pang of guilt crept up as I realized that these weren't your arms, Augustus. I gripped his bicep and gritted my teeth to harbor the pain shooting through my leg.

"I can walk," I said with a labored breath.

"No, you're not walking," he glanced at me before shifting his eyes to the front. He was breathing hard as he took hurried steps toward the bleachers. I forced my gaze to anywhere but his face.

Don't look up at him. Don't look up at him. I chanted in my mind not to look at the angry veins on his neck, the sheen of sweat gliding down his bare chest. Not to follow the path those beads of liquid took as they trickled down the bulge of his pectoral muscles and not to encourage the images of myself licking away those droplets through the expanse of his rippling abs.

God! Stop, Violet. It's wrong. Even worse when I knew they weren't for you. Those thoughts had to go away. I pushed them aside as he lowered me onto the bench.

"Is it hurting badly?" He asked, placing my ankle on his lap, and examining it. I winced as he touched the skin around the injury for tenderness and urged me to move it a little to check the extent of the damage. "I think you sprained your ankle. Thank God, it's not that bad."

"Umm- okay," I mumbled, willing myself to stop relishing the electrifying effect of his touch on my skin. He removed my shoes and socks, then pulled out a pain relief spray and ACE bandage from his sports bag. While I let him treat my pain, I stole a moment to admire the gentleness with which he sprayed and wrapped my ankle.

"Do you always carry this stuff?" I picked up the pain relief spray and waved it in front of his face. He was keeping up his long face.

"Yeah, we get a lot of twisted ankles and dislocated shoulders on the ground." He said, leaning back on the bench with his feet stretched out in front of him and my leg on his thigh as if it was the most natural thing to do. He pulled out a bottle from his bag and took a long sip.

"Adri, what's in that?" I pointed at the bottle.

"Why are you here, V? This is not your usual running schedule. Hell, you don't even run." He lifted the bottle to his lips and took another long sip, keeping his eyes on me.

I didn't answer. I removed the shoe from my other leg and placed it beside my sprained leg. It was the comfort of togetherness we both needed from each other, and I didn't want any awkward imagery to steal that away from us.

"How was the lunch with your father?" I snatched the bottle from his hand and took a hesitant sip. It certainly didn't taste like water or an energy drink. It tasted like the raw fire that burned my throat.

"What the fuck is this?" I rasped, coughing and hissing.

He gave me one of his smug smiles. "George Dickel Rye Whiskey, thank me later." He reached for the bottle and chuckled when I pulled it away. I took another sip and wiped my mouth with the back of my hand. "Easy baby, we don't want to get you drunk."

"Afraid that you can't handle my drunk self," I teased, taking another burning slug from the whiskey. I felt a little lightheaded after that round. The buzz helped in easing out some of the longings from my system.

"I can handle you very well," he said, tugging at my good ankle and pulling me a little closer to his side. He smelled of alcohol, sweat, and musky cologne. His eyes, the fiery green ones, piercing yet so soft. His fingers brushed mine for a millisecond as he secured the bottle from my hand and took a shot from the George Dickel Rye. "Only if you let me, V. Only if you let me."

His words reached the deepest darkest corner of my heart and burned like wildfire. As if his own words betrayed him, he looked away. He went chillingly still, chugging down the rest of the fiery liquid from the bottle. The same wildfire was behind his stark eyes and in the rigidness of his jaw.

We sat in silence for a while as he kept a firm hold on my legs and caressed my bandaged ankle. There were so many unsaid emotions between us.

"It went like shit," Adrian said. "My father thinks I shouldn't behave like a brat and accept that he has left us. Learn to live with the fact that my father has another son and wife to take care of. Make peace with knowing that he now comes with a package, a stepmother, and a stepbrother, non-negotiable. Fuck that shit! I never asked for this. Why won't he stop tormenting me and enjoy his new family?"

"He's your father, Adri," I said softly. His ears were red due to the strain on his muscles.

"When he let us go, he didn't even bother if we wanted him to stay." His throat bobbed, and his chest heaved. "He didn't even try, V. He just left and moved on as if it was easier than staying."

"I know, Adri. I know how it feels when you want someone to stay, but no matter what you do, they let you go." I was again back to the moment when you let me go when all I wanted was to stay. A silent sob rose and fell within me.

"Come here," he murmured, pulling me to his side. At that moment, as I rested my forehead under his chin and his arms circled my shoulders, I convinced myself that it was just a moment of comfort between us. It meant nothing more than those hugs we shared as teenagers. I forced myself to believe that I wanted those arms to be yours, Augustus.

But the moment my nose brushed through his bare neck and the smell of his skin caressed every corner of my soul- I forgot everything else. A powerful lightning bolt of energy zipped through me as he looked down at my face. I didn't want to tilt my head up and peer into his sea-green eyes, but my resolve failed as I finally did. I met his eyes, those sparkling green, beautiful eyes, drowning me in a whole new world.

So I let go, only this time it wasn't breaking my heart, it was healing my heart, and maybe that's what I needed, that's what I wanted. I tasted something familiar as my warm trembling lips brushed against the powerful heated desire of Adrian's Whiskey-scented lips. The briefest touch, an instant contact, that's all it accounted for as we both pulled away and detached ourselves from each other's warmth.

Suddenly, I felt a little underdressed as the heat of his body transferred to mine through the thin material of my tank top. And the awareness of my action rushed through me. Once again, the images of your dimpled smile flashed in front of my eyes. It followed a dash of guilt sliding down my spine.

"I'm so sorry," I stumbled backward, putting as much distance between us as possible. I slipped away from Adrian's arms, his comfort, his taste of familiarity.

"What the fuck did I do? I shouldn't have done that." He ran a hand through his messy brown hair, looking at me with boiling eyes, and the glint of hope in them made me scramble back on my feet. I shook my head and clenched my fists as a spear of pain skyrocketed through my sprained ankle, but the pain was good. It subsided the guilt and shame.

Adrian stood up, his arms reaching out to me, and then he held my shaking shoulders. "Don't apologize, V. Don't fucking ever apologize for that. You didn't do anything wrong. I'm in it too, and it didn't feel wrong to me."

I wrestled free. "No, it's wrong. You're my best friend and...no, just no." I turned, limping away as fast as possible, pushing past the web of messed-up emotions, running away from the feelings that weren't for you, Augustus.

Adrian followed me down the bleachers to the field and ran around to my front. His eyes burned with so many emotions as he stopped me with his hands on my shoulders. "It's not your fault to carry. I leaned in too, and I'm sorry if I crossed some lines. I don't know what happened there, but it wasn't wrong."

"No, there was a ton of wrong. How can I kiss you when-" I pushed Adrian's hands away from my shoulders and said in a cracked-up voice.

He went rigid. No more reaching out. "Say it, V. Finish that line."

My eyes turned glassy due to the unsaid passion radiating through his voice. "How can I kiss you when my heart belongs to Augustus?"

There was nothing left to say as I turned away, and he didn't stop me this time. I could feel his eyes on my back, but I didn't turn back. I couldn't turn back. Not when my heart was whirling in chaos.

"I know where your heart belongs but what I felt-" he yelled, making me pause for a fleeting second. "It wasn't wrong, V. I've never felt anything as right as that."

The power of his words was enough to push me off the edge, and I ran, limping, trembling. The moment I was in the comfort of my room, my resolve broke, and I closed my eyes to let out the warm salty drops from my eyes. And at that moment, I saw you, Augustus, your amber eyes delving deep into my soul, your hands slipping away from me with each of my backward steps.

That night deep in my sleep, I dreamed of your amber eyes caressing my skin with love. And then it was his sapphire green eyes unraveling me, piece by piece. I dreamed of his gentle touches igniting a fire I thought belonged to you. In my dream, he pulled me into his warmth again and kissed me as if I belonged to him, and that's when I woke up sweating, trembling with guilt.

So, I did what I had to do. I pushed that dream into one of the deepest darkest corners of my heart, locked away from my memories of you.

03 | Don't Play with Fire

I haven't seen Adrian since our confrontation at the cafeteria. It's good because it helps in forgetting the train of memories boiling in my head. I'm still processing the warnings he gave regarding Liam. Not that I haven't heard rumors, but I'm not putting my thoughts into his advances. That's the reason I've been ignoring his messages.

Unknown: Looking forward to meeting you at the party tonight.

That's the tenth message I've left unanswered, and I haven't even saved the guy's number. I'm in no way looking forward to meeting him at the party. The only thing that keeps coming into my mind whenever I think about Liam's party is the scowl on Adrian's face.

I don't know why he keeps doing this to me. Every time I decide to find someone decent enough to make me forget about how single I am, he scoops that opportunity out of my plate by either scaring the guy or by offering the guy a better alternative.

I blame my unavailable heart on you, Augustus, but my non-existent chances of casual hookups are all blamed upon Adrian. I keep my calculus notes aside and add Liam's number to my contacts list. Maybe after tonight, I might find something in the guy to keep him around.

"Is that Liam Parker from the soccer team?" Olivia snatches my phone and looks at the unattended messages, throwing herself on the couch beside me. "Bitch, I've had a crush on this dude since our freshman year."

With black hair and round-doe eyes, Oliva Hart gets a crush on everyone every year. But when it comes to her heart, none can own it except, of course, me. We've been together since the day of our orientation and have never left each other ever since. We're like sisters from different mothers, each other's therapists when we need one. When we moved out of the dorm into an apartment, she was the one who insisted on not having another girl in between us. Then when you have her as your soul sister, you need no one. After all, who would bear my messiness, my zero cooking skills, and my unholy sleep cycles? It's only Olivia for me, quite literally.

I raise my eyebrow in question, and a grin appears on my lips. "Last time I checked, you had a crush on Noah."

Olivia rolls her eyes, tossing my phone on my lap. "I have a crush on Noah now, but I have had a crush on Liam since we watched him play soccer for the first time. But he never once took my flirting seriously. And here he's giving you his full attention, yet you decide to ignore him."

"Can you blame me? The guy's a predator, and I'm his next prey. Makes up a good reason to ignore him." I rest my legs on the edge of the couch and my head on her shoulder.

"Says who? Adrian?" She has a suggestive smile on her lips, and I close my eyes, nodding. "You know, he's just a jealous prick."

My mind goes back to the moment between us in the cafeteria- How Adrian's fiery green eyes burned me inside as Liam typed in his number on my phone. His warm breath glided like molten lava on my skin as he warned me to be away from Liam. I once again clear my thoughts before they can make my skin tingly.

"Why would he be jealous?" I clear my throat and wiggle my head down to her lap. "He's an obnoxious prick."

Olivia laughs. "Seriously, Vio. You know that's bullshit. He is a jealous obnoxious prick, period."

"He's not jealous," I shake my head, looking up at her gray eyes. "There's no reason for him to be jealous over me getting asked by Liam."

"Because he doesn't want you to date anyone else. Isn't that obvious?"

"You're delusional. Nothing is obvious except the fact that I don't date. You know I don't." I groan, rubbing my face with my hands. "Are you coming to the party with me?"

"Is Adrian going to be there?" She has a devilish grin, and I know it calls for trouble.

I roll my eyes. "What, you have a crush on Adrian now?"

"Maybe," she shrugs. "Someone has to tap that hot piece of abs."

I remain silent, trying to shake off the burning sensation her words created in my throat. I know girls from all years fangirl over Adrian's ocean-green eyes, his messy brown hair complementing his sharp cheekbones and the deep timbre of his voice.

"Please don't fuck my best friend, Liv, or we're no more cuddling together." I give her a warning look and get off her lap.

"Can I at least have first base with him?" Olivia makes fake pleading eyes, fluttering her eyelashes playfully. That earns her a cushion on the face, and we end up into a fit of laughter. But my mind doesn't stop picturing Olivia kissing Adrian. It sets every corner of my soul on fire.

***

In the afternoon, Olivia decides to take the initiative for the grocery shopping and convinces me to follow her to the supermarket. At first, I wanted to refuse her and finish working on my presentation for the coming week. But when I think about how I had been lying on the couch for hours, I decide I might as well go for a walk, or else I won't be able to get creative.

When we arrive at the supermarket, Olivia starts stocking our baskets with snacks and beverages. Since it's a warm day outside, I'm wearing a light spaghetti top and skirt, which explains the goosebumps on my arms as I collect the packs of yogurts from the freezer aisle. I go through the back of a frozen green peas packet when my eyes capture someone familiar.

Freshly showered dark brown hair, a well-known fragrance of aftershave and body wash, makes me squeeze the package of green peas I'm holding.

I remain stunned for a few seconds as Adrian comes around the corner. I did not expect to meet him here. He's wearing gray sweatpants and a white T-shirt that hugs his broad shoulders perfectly. Our eyes finally meet, and I can see the same surprise on his face as he reaches out for the pack of crisps on the opposite aisle.

I step away from the freezer, running my fingers through my wild hair.

He watches me as he fills up his shopping basket, his eyes unexpectedly unshielded like a blizzard as they take in every dip and curve of my body, lingering a little longer on my exposed collarbones.

His green eyes work as fireworks on my insides, and I take a heaving breath to push the heaviness in my chest away.

"Adrian," I say, stuffing my basket with random snacks.

The look on his face is priceless as he blinks and clears his throat. He appears confused about his shockingly wild way of checking me out.

"Hey, you," Adrian manages to mumble, looking at me slightly in surprise. "What a coincidence."

What a coincidence, indeed. I'm not sure how to conceal my reluctance to look or speak.

"Can't believe they ran out of raisin cookies!" Olivia jumps to my side just in time to save my day. Her expression changes from grumpy to one of excitement as she sees Adrian. She puts her lips next to my ear and says, "How does he look so hot all the time?"

I choke on my saliva with the sudden sultry husk in her voice, and I jab an elbow in her stomach to shut her up. To my relief, Adrian doesn't look up and hopefully doesn't hear Liv's naked confession of his sexiness. He moves to the next aisle and gives me a chance to pull Olivia to the side. I close my eyes and look at her in disbelief.

"Can you at least lower your voice while making such comments?" I shake my head.

"What's wrong with harmless flirting? Adrian is our friend. He won't mind." She says, leering at his backside shamelessly. "I want to see his angry face, like right now."

"Wha-" before I can figure out what's going on in her rogue mind, she rushes over to another aisle.

I curse under my breath and make my way to the self-service checkout, carrying both baskets. Of course, Liv left her basket with me. When I reach the rows of checkout machines, Adrian appears on the one beside me. My breath hitches when his unpredictable eyes move in my direction as we wait for our turns in the line.

He looks away as Liv returns to my side. I give her a skeptical look as she winks at me and drops a black package in my basket. My eyes widen when I look down at the pack of condoms in my basket.

"What - What the fuck, Liv?" I gape at her.

"Please let me have my fun, Vio." She whispers as I quickly secure the pack before my turn comes, shoving it back on her palm.

"I don't need it." I start unloading my basket of various snack packets with some groceries on the side.

She clicks her tongue and whispers in a low voice. "Don't you want to exact Adrian's controlling ass? Give him some taste of his cockiness. It will be fun."

I follow her gaze and instantly realize what childish pranks are brewing in her head. For a moment, I think of refusing to partake in her mischief, then the idea of exacting Adrian's controlling ass seems like fun.

Maybe, I'll regret it later, but I don't think twice as I take the black package from Liv's hand and scan it on the machine, making sure Adrian's eyes follow as I place it in the bagging area.

Adrian looks at the black package, and his fiery green eyes are on my face. A thunderous scowl appears on his face, and his jaw turns rigid.

As I continue scanning the rest of the groceries in my basket, he never once shifts his eyes from me. His red ears and tight shoulders are evidence enough of his anger.

I leave Liv at the checkout and storm out of the shop, trying to avoid his burning gaze. Once I reach my car in the parking lot, I relax. The idea of pissing Adrian off seemed easy in my head, but it's way too intense to put into practice. As I drop the groceries in the backseat and close the door, his strong arms come on either side of my head.

I swallow a gasp as my back collides against the car and the smell of Adrian's aftershave invades my senses. He breathes heavily, his face just an inch away from mine, and my eyes take in the tempting view of his magnificent neck.

"Why do you need these?" He asks, exasperated, reaching through into my shopping bag and pulling out the black package.

"Why do people need condoms, Adri?" I scoff at him, trying hard not to cower away.

His hands turn red with the pressure as he leans some more, clouding me, and for some weird reason, I like our closeness.

"I don't give a fuck about people. Why do you need these?" He asks coldly.

I fist my hands on my sides as his warm breath tickles my skin and spreads pleasurable tingles all over my body. It can't be happening. I shouldn't feel like this near him.

"I might need it now that I'm planning to date Liam." I glare at him, trying to push him away, but he catches my arm and places it on the side of my head.

"If he touches as much as a hair of yours, I will-" Adrian grits, his voice a little growly.

"You will what, Adri?"

"You'll see." He releases my hand and backs away as fast as he crowds me. At some point, one of the straps of my spaghetti top falls off my shoulder, but I only notice it when he secures it back. Goosebumps appear on my skin due to the soft caresses of his fingertips.

As I stay plastered to the door of my car, he takes a few backward steps flashing me a smug grin.

"Thanks for this, by the way," he holds up the black package and looks at it with a smirk. "Since you spent so generously on it, someone should use it. After all, it would be a waste if we don't."

I look at him in utter disbelief and feel like punching his face, but he doesn't give me a chance and walks away.

"You're an asshole, Adri!" I shout at his disappearing figure and kick the tire of my car, wincing afterward.

04 | Need to Move On

It's an open house party. The random swarm of boys and girls keeps sweeping through the front door, and I recognize most of them from the university. The house gets crowded every minute, the air hazy with smoke. I'm already suffocating, if not the crowd, definitely due to the look Adrian is giving me.

Since I arrived at the party, Liam has been away from me, standing by his captain. Of course, that's what Adrian does. He keeps sabotaging my chances with guys like Liam. No strings attached, no commitment type. But I don't want anything other than that, either. I've tried falling for the other; it left me with a sore heart. The love which lasts forever, I can't imagine having that with anyone who isn't you, Augustus.

Then there's this ugly anxiety in my chest that keeps howling from within. In the evening, while I was getting ready for the party, my mom called. She had an unexpected edge to her voice. It almost made my heartbeat stop. Her desperate sighs turned my stomach, and I wanted everything to shut down. But then, when she said we were still waiting for the test results, I felt my heart start beating again.

"They want to do another MRI tomorrow morning," Mom's voice was shaky and low. "It's still too early to confirm- if it's a tumor or not. Your dad seems to disregard the possibility, but I'm scared."

I swallow the lump forming in my throat and press a hand against my chest to subside the dull ache. I hope my dad's test results turn out negative. He's too young to have a fatal illness. I want him to be there when I need my dad. I need him in every important decision in my life, and I want him to be healthy. Mom and Daisy need him.

The thick feeling crawls up my throat. I force myself to find anything among the flickering green and red neon lights, the smell of alcohol, the booming noise of the bass, and bodies moving, grinding against each other, but nothing takes away the pain. Not even the electrifying vibrations of the music thumping through my bones.

The world around me swirls faster, and I feel tangled up in a heap of chaotic emotions. I shouldn't have agreed to be here. It's not the place or time for me to be here. Parties had never been my choice of places, but with one look at the girl across the hall, dancing and laughing through her heart, one could tell there was nowhere else Olivia would rather be.

My fingers fist on the soft fabric of the wrap dress I'm wearing. Olivia chose this dress for me, a little too perfectly hugging the dips and curves of my body, exposing enough skin around my neck and thigh down. I would have never agreed to wear it if it wasn't in a shade of deep violet.

I look down at the punch in my solo cup, and I assume it has been spiked, but without giving it another thought, I gulp it down in one go. The burning sensation that follows isn't enough to take away the panic grating against my heart and mind. When I move to the back corner of the room, I feel the warm salty liquid dripping down my cheek, and I wipe it with the back of my hand. I can't lose my shit in public.

Save it for later.

The first person my eyes search for comfort is the boy with an everlasting scowl on his face, a messy brown tuft sitting haphazardly on his head, the black T-shirt hugging his broad shoulder perfectly, paired with black jeans. A black chain hangs down his neck with the dog tag necklace. My lips tip upward with the knowledge that it's my gift he's wearing tonight. The one I gave him on his twenty-first birthday, one year back when we were still in each other's comfort.

Oh, God! I crave his comfort every single day. As I stand awkwardly against the wall, I wish he would walk toward me and let me know I'm not alone. Why do I always crave people I love to stay by my side when they don't want to?

As an add-on to my misery, I watch Charlotte brushing past me intentionally and going straight to the soccer team. The moment she looks over her shoulder and gives me one of her mean-girl smirks, I feel like showing her my middle finger, but I give her a tight-lipped smile instead. The image of her kissing Adrian on his cheek after the last game flashes in front of my eyes. She bends down, holding the back of the couch, and kisses his cheek the same way. My eyes lock into his green ones as Charlotte says something in his ear and sits on his lap.

Charlotte looks stunning tonight with her long blonde hair and finely curved body. My chest feels itchy as she caresses his chin, and I don't know why I turn away from looking any further. It feels like a double standard for him to stop me from dating Liam when he's all touchy so openly with every other girl who throws herself at him. I take a moment to gather my emotions, releasing a deep breath that's still stuck in my throat.

The speaker blares the latest pop song. The sharp volume accompanied by the trip result of another two shots of spiked punch makes my head hum with the music. I rest my head backward on the wall for a second when a pair of bulky arms wrap around my waist.

"Liam!"

"Sorry, beautiful, for making you wait so long," he slurs out and doesn't give me enough time to react as he turns me around, hugs me tightly, lifting me off the ground.

"Liam, please put me down now!" I shout in his ear, music making it difficult to capture the edge in my voice. I'm beyond shocked by his sudden closeness, but I try to excuse him just this once.

I place my arms on his shoulders as he gets me back on my feet, and behind him, I notice Adrian. He's off the couch, Charlotte brushing her hair in confusion and looking at him as he glares in my direction.

Liam tips his head in front of me and grins. "I wanted to have a moment with you alone since you arrived at the party. This dress looks so sinful. You've no idea how much I regret not asking you out sooner."

I've no mind whatever he says, but I give him a small smile. "You haven't asked me out yet. You invited me to your house party and then ignored me all evening. I think it's rude."

We walk over to the drinks table and grab another set of punches. Liam drinks from his cup and leans closer to my ear, brushing my hair away from my shoulder. "Give me a chance to rectify that."

Liam puts my drink down and drags me onto the dance floor. And not a moment later, I see Adrian on the floor with an over-excited Charlotte dancing around him. She's moving her slender frame sensually, grinding herself on his front.

I lose my mind, not sure what's the reason for this sudden fire that's surging through my nerves. It's a combination of both past and present. The night of the fundraiser reels in my mind as I sway to the music. I remember how my eyes were on you, Augustus, as I danced for you to watch, then later how you broke Jamie's nose for trying to kiss me forcefully.

As music infiltrates my hazy mind, I remember how that night we kissed. It was my first kiss, you're my first kiss, Augustus, and I wanted you to be my first in everything. But that was the night when you broke my heart too. You left me, Augustus, and my heart never stopped loving you, even after all this time. I need to stop myself from reliving the memories over and over again. It hurts so much. I want to move on, Augustus, or fail while trying.

I feel Liam's body against my back, his arms circle my waist, and we get consumed in smoke.

He takes me away from the dance floor to the far end of the hall, and I wonder if Adrian is watching or if he is too busy dirty dancing with Charlotte. I've nothing in my mind except the caving pain in my chest and desperation to feel anything except heartbroken. So, when he pulls me into one of the dimly lit rooms, I let him. But the moment his half-lid eyes roam around my body, I break free from his hold and wander into the room.

It's a typical college boy's room with a queen-size bed that occupies half the space inside, a dresser on the far end wall, and a desk with all the electronic equipment. A sudden wave of nausea hits me, and I sit on the bed for a second.

As I whirl around to check on the guy who came in with me, he closes the door and faces me with a lopsided grin. My heart jumps up to my throat, and suddenly it feels like the most stupid decision of my life. But then, there isn't anywhere else I would rather be. The thought of going downstairs and watching Charlotte grinding her hips against Adrian makes my gut twist in a tangled knot; neither does drowning in anxiety over my father's health condition seem so appealing. And then the memory of you is a no-go for me. So, I'll take my chances with Liam. After all, this is what I want. I want to move on from this love that keeps hurting me.

"It's not my room," Liam says. "It's my brother's, and I didn't lock the door. So, you can relax."

He takes slow steps towards the bed, and I shift towards the farthest end, my legs hanging from the edge. I need a little space and time to reconsider everything.

"This is the only place your bodyguard won't forsake our chance to form a connection." He winks, but it only enrages me.

"Don't call him that. He's my best friend and has every right to be mindful of me." I wipe my sweaty palms on my lap as anxiety floods my mind.

"I never had to wait so long to ask out a girl. If it were not for Adrian, I already had you." He raises a brow at me and sits beside me on the bed. "I've never put this much effort into any girl. Girls usually don't even wait to be asked out."

"Well, you experienced something new then." I grit out a smile.

"Violet," he leans a little closer. "This is why I go crazy when I look at you."

I already dread the idea of letting him have my company. The anxiety of not having any experience with guys is unavoidable as the heat of his body inches closer.

It's normal.

Just give him a chance.

You can do it.

God! I can't do this.

When he places his hand on my thigh over my flimsy dress, I immediately know it's not what I want. My body goes cold and rigid as his fingers run up and down my thigh, a little bolder this time. I snap my head in his direction, knowing he isn't the guy who cares about consent.

"Liam," I warn, placing my hand on his in a firm grip. "Please take your hand off of me."

He smirks, holding my wrist with the other hand, and moves his hand up to my hips. "Stop playing hard to get. I know this is what you want. Let's stop bullshitting about dating and all."

Every cell in my body repulses him, dread seeps through my fibers, and I tense up when his face dips down to my neck. As I grind my teeth, bracing myself to work on my defenses, he suddenly flies off the bed and onto the floor. It takes me a minute to recollect my senses and connect with whatever happened. My eyes go from Liam to the familiar six feet, two inches frame looming over him. From his deadly green eyes to his messy dark hair, Adrian looks intimidating as hell. All I can see is his back, his muscles tense, and his body stiff.

"Get your fucking hands off of her, Parker!" Adrian bellows, pulling him back on his feet with a hold on his shirt's collar. "Didn't I warn you to behave?"

Adrian's temper is a hot topic around the college, and everyone who knew him knew better than to mess up with his head. But here's Liam, who is comparatively lean and less built, going after me. Of course, it's his doom right there.

"What the fuck, man! She wanted it too," Liam yells, trying to wriggle out of his hold.

Adrian snaps his head towards me, his eyes brimming with fiery disapproval, and the way he stares at me, I almost feel like digging a hole to bury myself.

"Look, man, if you guys are an item, just put that out in the open," Liam says, running a hand through his wild hair. "And if you guys are friends with benefits, then it shouldn't be a problem if I have her too."

I get approximately two seconds to process Liam's words before Adrian's fist slams across his face.

"Goddammit!" Liam falls against the wall, holding his bleeding nose.

I cover my mouth as a gasp escapes and dash towards the angry, feral hunk of a guy, holding his shoulder to stop him from landing another punch at Liam.

"Adri, stop it! You already broke his nose." I glare at him.

"Get the fuck away from my face and consider yourself benched for the next game!" Adrian shifts his fiery gaze to me. "I said if he touched you as much as one of your hair, I'd finish him off."

"Why? Only you have the privilege to get touches from Charlotte."

"What does Charlotte have to do with this?"

"Everything. So, you can date whoever you want and touch whoever you like, and I can't do the same. Maybe, I did want to be with Liam."

I hear a grunt as Liam curses under his breath, holding on to his broken nose, slams the door shut, and rushes out of the room. I have zero sympathy for him, though. He deserved that punch for being a non-consensual prick.

"Well, congratulations on getting your control back on my life," I grit out, jabbing my index finger into his chest. "You finally succeeded in crossing Liam out of my dating list. And now, most likely, no one will ever want to be near me. They will either tag me as your fuck buddy or be scared to get their nose broken by you."

He stares into my wild eyes, and I have to gulp down due to the dark look on his face. The flush on his face as he glares down at my finger pressed to his chest makes me pull my hand away. His fingers latch around my wrist, and I'm backed up against the wall.

I shudder under the heat radiating off his taut body as, in two strides, he's on me, our chest just an inch away from touching. My breath quickens, and my body goes rigid. I press my back against the wall as his hand tightens around my wrist, and then something shifts in him. He's heaving, and his warm breath hits my face every time he exhales. I can see him losing his control altogether. "Why, V? Why do you need someone like Liam when your heart belongs to goldilocks?"

His words hit home, and I can't hold back the tears trailing down my eyes. "I want to move on, Adri. Can't you see I'm tired of waiting? But also, I can't stop loving Augustus. So, yeah, I'm miserable. I'm so fucking miserable that I let Liam kiss me."

The moment those words leave my mouth, his jaw goes rigid, and I swallow hard, looking into the raging depths of his eyes.

"Fuck!" He curses, gnashing his teeth, and his fist lands beside my head. "Where did he kiss you?"

I blink at him in confusion for a second but try to back away from his closeness. "On my neck, but it doesn't concern you, Adri."

His nostrils go wild with anger before he touches his nose to my neck. "God, I can smell him on your skin, and it so damn concerns me."

I should be pushing him away, but the moment his warm breath touches my skin, I'm on fire. Electrifying energy pulls me towards his light feathery touch as his nose keeps tracing a pulse on my neck. He releases my wrist, placing both his hands on the wall beside my head, his face still on my neck.

My heart races fiercely. My hands fist Adrian's T-shirt around his shoulders to keep our chests from crashing against each other. I have never felt something so powerful like this, and my insides start burning up, throbbing with need. The worst part is I know it's not how you should feel around your best friend or someone who isn't in your heart. "Adri."

He releases a ragged breath against my neck and rests his forehead against my shoulder. "I can smell Liam on your skin and Augustus in your heart."

Dread knots in my stomach. Adrian's words feel like a sharp blade slashing my skin.

He steps away from my body, taking the warm and fuzzy feelings with him. My throat feels constricted as his icy gaze locks with mine, devoid of all the passion I saw in them a moment ago. He clenches his fists to his sides. I don't give him the time to apologize as I walk past him, away from his comfort, from something new and substantial.

Because Adrian is right, my heart still smells like you, Augustus, and I don't know what my soul smells like from this point onwards.

05 | Friends Again?

I need to walk away from Adrian. It's the only way to settle the chaos in my mind. The party continues to rage on as I squeeze my way through the sweaty crowd on the dance floor. My eyes search for a familiar black-haired, doe-eyed girl, but Olivia is nowhere around. I punch in her number with my trembling fingers, not pausing until I'm outside Liam's house. I wait for her to pick up my call, but she doesn't. I try again..

Still no response.

My patience wears out, and I type in a quick text to her.

Me: I'm heading home. Be safe.

I know she will be safe since she's with Noah. Apart from Adrian, the only decent guy on the soccer team is their keeper, Noah.

The cool night air hits my face, followed by cold drizzling rain splatters as I step on the street. The clouds grumble above me, breaking the last of my resolve. A shiver travels down the length of my body, and I hug my arms around myself. The icy raindrops find their way beneath the thin fabric of my dress, making it difficult not to feel the chills in my bones.

My stomach feels heavy once again with the realization of my sloppy behavior. Instead of dealing with my problems with an open and positive mind, I decided to get drunk and put myself in a questionable situation with a guy I hardly knew. I think about the worst that could've happened tonight if Adrian wouldn't be there for me.

With a stealing breath, I gather my senses which aren't under the haze of alcohol and hop across the street. It's almost midnight, and this side of the road, with the brick house along the line, is relatively quiet. I don't know why I'm walking in the rain, drenched from head to toe and trembling, but somehow it helps me get rid of the bone-crushing anxiety.

After a few thoughtless strides, I hear the engine purring behind me. The thundering sound of the motorcycle is enough for me to guess who is riding it. I squeeze my eyes and keep walking as his approach gets louder. He motors towards me at speed only he can manage to straddle the beast of a motorbike and halts on the curb beside me.

I spin around to spot Adrian. His eyes are on my face as he turns off the engine and steps out of the bike. The black T-shirt clings to his muscular torso, dripping sodden under the rain. I try to ignore the messy brown hair that falls in sexy soaked strands across his brow as he takes off his helmet, but I fail as he stands in front of me with a deep frown.

"What the hell are you doing, V?"

"Walking home." I spit through clattering teeth.

He releases a scowl, looking at me with commanding eyes. "Well, get on the bike. I will drop you."

I blink through the freezing drizzle. "I don't want to. Please leave me alone, Adri. I can't handle your obnoxious self at the moment."

He steps closer to me, pushing back some of his wet hair. "I'm only trying to protect you."

"Don't you get it? I don't want you to be my knight in shining armor."

"I'm sorry, V."

My head jerks back with the sudden softness in his voice. I've heard him speak to me in that tone ages ago. "I don't want your apology, Adri. Just let me be. You have no idea how I'm feeling right now."

"Then tell me. Talk to me." He whispers, brushing away a salty trail with his thumb. His eyes, which somehow resemble the green apple candy, and how he can see my tears against the rain, flutter my heart. But I pull away from his touch.

My lung seizes, and I swipe my tongue on my wobbly lips as anxiety creeps through me, sudden and uncontrolled. Adrian's fingers are gentle as he brushes them against my wet cheeks and holds my face in both of his palms.

"Can't you see, our friendship is falling apart, V?" He leans in, his green eyes begging me for attention. "It kills me to see you like this and not be able to give you comfort. When did we stop being friends?"

I shake my head, and my throat jams, choking my voice. "Don't you know when and why?"

He squeezes his eyes, and when he finally looks at me, I see the same sea of emotions as mine. "If it's because of the kiss we shared a year ago, then it doesn't have to be the reason. Let's not make it a big deal. It was just a peck on the lips, a friendly kiss. Forget whatever bullshit I said about feelings and all."

"What are you saying, Adri? I don't understand." I scan his face in confusion.

"I can kiss you right now. The same way we kissed that day on the bleachers. And it won't mean anything." He has a playful glint in his eyes.

"Wasn't one kiss enough to create problems in our friendship? You want to repeat that awkward moment." I scoff, glaring at him. The memory of his whiskey-scented lips lingers in my mind, creating a chain of crazy emotions.

"I want to clear things out between us. We can recreate the memory, but this time with no awkwardness or confused feelings. Maybe we can forget whatever we felt and move back to the way we were before that kiss." He looks at my lips for a flickering moment, and then his eyes look back at me for approval.

"What if it turns into another disaster and destroys everything still left of us?" My voice is as small as it could be.

"It won't, I promise." He speaks. "At that moment, we were vulnerable, but now we're in our senses."

I think through every word he says, and my mind wants to get rid of all the confusing emotions I share with him. He is right. Every dent in our friendship started with that one kiss. Not a kiss, just a peck. A friendly peck between friends. I want to test out his theory. It will either erase the memory or solidify the new feelings that are beginning to take shape.

"Okay, a peck then." My teeth clatter again, and my voice is a little shaky.

Adrian brushes the pad of his thumb on my cheekbones with a soft endearing smile and gives me a reassuring nod.

And then, as the icy drizzle pours down on us from the splitting sky, his head leans forward, his fingers tuck my hair behind my ear while his soft, pillowy lips touch mine. A sudden fiery brush of his lips electrocutes all my nerve endings, sucks the air out of my lungs, and leaves a trail of fire on my lips.

It's a peck, as he would like to say, lasting only a second before he leans away as if another second would be a gamble of control from his side.

If I had refused this chance a few minutes ago, I would've missed this friendly peck between friends with a handsome hunk of a guy with ocean eyes and sunshine of a smile.

If I can keep the memories of his whiskey-scented lips in the deepest darkest corner of my heart, then I can push this fiery kiss in the rain into some empty dark corner as well, only that I can't. Every space that lived in silence starts echoing this feeling. Heat flames my skin as I stare at his soft fiery lips that branded me as they pressed to mine in a stupor.

I want them back on my lips.

This time I want to burn in their scorching heat as I part them with mine and taste the secret inside them. I want to leave my taste in every nook and cranny of Adrian's mouth so that he can never replace it with any Charlotte. I want to sift my fingers through his messy brown hair and explore the depths of it. I want to flatten my palm on the expanse of those abs under his black T-shirt and feel them flex under my touch. I want to do all of these and so much more.

But I can't do it.

I shouldn't do it.

Not when he looks at me with hope in those calm eyes that it means nothing more than a peck.

"See, we didn't feel anything." He croaks out, taking away his touch from my face and wiping the trails of rain from his face.

I remain stunned for a few seconds before lying to him with a nod. "Yes, no feelings at all."

A confident lie we both share now.

I can read the pleadings in his eyes as they lock momentarily with mine.

I'm sorry I couldn't keep my promise. We messed it up again. Fucking epic this time.

"Let's never do that again." He says over his shoulder as he walks over to the bike.

"Yes, never again," I mumble as I follow him.

Because if we do this again, I might end up embarrassing myself by severing the lines of our friendship.

I can feel a pinch in my heart with the remembrance of my first kiss, the kiss I shared with you, Augustus. I'm losing the feel of your touch, and it's breaking my heart.

I wish you were here.

I wish Adrian wouldn't be here.

But the truth is he's here, and you're not.

He unhooks a second helmet from the bike and turns around, holding it out for me. With a determination to set everything right between us and a softness in his eyes, this is the green-eyed boy with whom I grew up. I share so many happy moments and sad ones with this boy. A frenzy of emotions shoots through me as he sighs, setting his helmet on the seat and adjusting mine on my head. He gathers my wet hair to one side carefully. His fingertips leave a trail of goosebumps as they glide across my neck and the side of my face.

"We still have to work out all the missing days of our friendship." I place my hands over the helmet to adjust my small skull, and he buckles the strap.

He scowls at me. "Maybe, you missed, but I was always watching over you like your guardian angel."

"More like a creep."

He chuckles, putting his helmet back on and straddling the bike. "That was me being an angel. My creepy self is a whole other thing. We don't want to go there, do we?"

"I have seen all of you. Remember the summer you dropped your towel, and I saw your naked butt?" I grin at him. That was the summer we went to the beach for a family vacation.

"Don't remind me what I saw that summer when the waves almost plunged you in, and I saved you." His rumbling timbre stills me in my place. His voice is a cloud of smoke, his breath a potent elixir.

The smug smile on his lips says it all, and I've no idea what exactly he saw that day. The only thing I remember while choking on the salty water as it stung my eyes and nose is Adrian carrying me out of the water in his arms. When I regained my senses, I was wrapped in a fluffy towel, and he was stroking my wet hair, looking all pale.

"You never told me what you saw exactly. So, it doesn't count." I spit, placing my hand on his tight muscles, and slither up behind him. "You're too chicken to remind me."

"Are you sure you want to know?" He angles his head over his shoulder as I squeeze my thighs around his hip. The dress slides up a little, making it difficult not to feel his body heat through the rough material of his jeans. I can feel his muscles tense, like mine, but he shifts his attention to the gears, turning us through the drizzly wind. He moves his hand back, holds my cold fingers, and wraps them around his waist, making me snuggle some more to his back. "I don't think so. But I can assure you one thing - it was way sexier than my naked butt."

That earns him a tickle on his belly, and we laugh like crazy as he zooms toward my apartment. I feel every twitch, every contraction of his muscle plastered on his back as he rides the bike through the turns. The purring of the engine transfers his excitement to me. It's the first time I'm on his motorcycle since he owned the black beast, but somehow I don't feel frightened as he shifts the gears and maneuvers it. It almost feels like the only escape from my troubled mind. With him, it's always like this, natural and instinctual. I'm content snuggled up against his body heat as the icy cold wind breezes around us.

***

Adrian trails after me as soon as I open my apartment door. I leave him wandering around my place and praise Olivia in my mind for clearing up my clutter from the living area. What can I say? I'm not a very organized human. I grab a bottle of water from the fridge on my way to the bedroom and toss it to him after chugging a mouthful.

"You should get changed," he says, twisting the cap back on, placing the bottle on the counter, and leaning against the island. "Take a shower."

Of course, because apparently, I smell like Liam.

"Why? Because I smell like Liam?" My blood simmers, and I shoot daggers through my eyes as I shake my head and glare at him. I grab a clean towel from the heap of unfolded mess in my dresser, but when I turn around to throw it at his face, I find his gaze narrowing at my question.

"No, because you drenched in the rain," he says, leaning against the door jamb of my bedroom, "And I'm pretty sure you no more smell like him."

"Yeah, how are you so sure now?"

"After being plastered to my back the entire ride, I'm pretty sure you smell like me now." He steps a foot inside, takes the towel from my hands, and drifts back into the living room. All the while, his green eyes held me in a daze, veering electricity up my spine.

I feel my heart pinching again with a possibility I know shouldn't be there. I strip and let my heartbeat drown in the spurting water of the shower. It would be better if Adrian's words or anything related to him didn't affect me, except it does. I try washing away all the new feelings he's stirring in me and all the sinful things my mind keeps brewing up every time I look into his eyes.

With us pretending to ignore whatever this feeling is, it will be difficult not to be uncomfortable around each other. But I'm going to work on that friendship as we promised. That's what keeps bugging my head as I step out and change into a pair of sweatpants and a baggy shirt.

I sigh in relief that I'm not in a towel as soon as I step out of the bathroom. Because I find Adrian on my unmade bed, sitting over my tangled-up sheets, talking on the phone. He ends it with a goodnight and looks up at me with a sudden softness in his voice.

"I was talking to Sarah." He says, straightening his spine and getting up from my bed. "You weren't responding to her messages. That's why she freaked out."

My stomach tightens with the same anxiety I've been pushing away. I ignore Adrian's eyes as I walk out of the room, finger-combing my wet hair.

"Why didn't you tell me about your father?" He asks, following me into the hall. Of course, my mom informed him about my father's health condition, and now he's trying to pity my anxiety or maybe lecture me on not sharing it with him. Sometimes, I feel his friendship with my mom overpowers my friendship with him.

He grips the back of the couch where I flop down and watches me stabbing in random channels on the television.

"We were not talking." I shrug, pausing on Nat Geo and increasing the volume. There's a long pause, almost like he disappeared from the room, but he snatches the TV remote from my hand and mutes it.

"I'm not here to pity you, V." His timbre is soft as he stands tall before me with his hands on his hips, forcing me to look up at him instead of the muted screen.

Why is he still here? He should leave. My eyes dart toward the open window across the room, and I groan when I see it's still raining outside. I can't push him out of my apartment in this weather.

He's here bare-chested with the dog tag necklace falling sexily down his neck and black metal complimenting his tan skin. Textured brown hair falls rebelliously over his brow as he looks down at me with those ocean-green eyes. His black jeans hang low on his sculpted hips, giving a nice view of the sharp patterns of his muscle and the dark dusting of hair below his navel. He's arresting in a not-so-demanding yet challenging way that makes it easy to dive into his glory.

"Stop looking at me like that, V." He settles down on the couch moving my legs to the side.

"Like what?" I ask, placing my legs on his lap and leaning my head against the armrest. I do know what look he is talking about, but I feel rather smug, making his ear tips turn red. He can be cute too, when he is shy, and I'm glad that look is reserved for me alone.

"If you're trying to divert our topic of discussion, then you're failing." His eyes are hard this time when I meet his gaze, his jaw has a tightness, and I know he hates it when I close off from him. "I'm here, V, and not because I pity you. I'm here because I care. I thought you were doing fine with your job at the coffee house and going to the dance classes, but I was wrong, wasn't I?"

My eyes itch with each of his words and turn glassy as I nod, picking on my nails. "You were not talking to me, Adri."

"Come here," he says quietly, softly, and an outstretched hand appears beneath my face.

I stare at his hands for a few seconds, contemplating the comfort and security that comes with them. When I finally place my cold palms on his warm ones, certainty replaces unpredictability. When he pulls me to his side and brushes his fingers through my tangled waves, I realize it's worth all the walls that are cracking inside right at this moment. And taking a final leap of faith, I rest my head on his chest, suppressing the moan of relief his scent forces from me, and move close enough to rest my legs on his lap.

"I'm sorry for being such a bad friend." He cups the back of my neck. "I'll never do that again. And you have to promise not to close me off when you're sad. These sad flickers in your brownie eyes. I hate it."

His words stick inside my throat, making it tighten with the passion radiating from his voice.

"I think we both need to work on this," I say, "but I know we'll ace it if we try."

He props his chin on my head and whispers, "I'm with you, V, always."

We stay on the couch for a long time before my phone chimes up with a notification. It's a message from Olivia.

Liv: Tell me you reached safely. I'll be a little late, but I'm safe. Noah is with me. ;)

Me: I'm home and safe. Stay sober and be nice to Noah. ;)

Adrian leans back on the couch, staring at me as I type in the message and toss my phone on the trunk.

"She'll be safe with Noah, right?" I ask.

"Noah's a decent guy. The real concern here is will he be safe with Olivia?" He gives me one of his infamous smirks as he stands, tucking his hands inside the front pockets of his jeans. "I should go."

"Stay," my voice is a little rushed, and I cringe internally for sounding so desperate. My eyes roam from Adrian's sparkling green eyes to his exposed torso and back up. "Are you going to head out like that?"

"Are we going to watch a movie or something if I stay?" He crosses his arms across his chest and raises a brow in my direction. I can read in his eyes that he never intended to leave but wanted me to ask him to stay. He's back to being *the obnoxious Adrian.*

"What movie?" I ask him, brushing away the waves of my tangled hair falling over my eyes and nose.

"*All the Bright Places.*" He grabs the remote and unmutes the television. He rents the movie and sets it up on the screen, giving me a show of his back muscles flexing as he moves.

"I told you not to look at me like that." He says, joining me on the couch and pressing the play button on the remote.

"Why did you choose this movie?" I chew on the inside of my cheek. "You don't like cheeky teen romances."

He settles beside me, propping his feet on the trunk and stretching his arm along the back of the couch behind me. Then his heated gaze captures my throat as I gulp visibly and back to my eyes. "Because it has a Violet in it."

My pulse spikes as the movie starts, and he faces the screen as if he can see right through me but decides to avoid it. So, I do the same and let my focus shift to the TV screen.

"I want to do something else, too, if you'll allow me." His voice is soft under the loud dialogue of the movie.

Something else, what? Kiss me? Pull me on your lap, smell the column of my neck, and let me do the same. God! Tell me that's not what you want to do.

"What?" My voice turns dry and hoarse with all the dirty possibilities wiring in my head. I'm burning up all of a sudden.

His fingers brush the skin of my shoulder softly, up, down, and in a circle. The cool metal of his rings against my heated skin zigs electricity up my spine as he takes forever to speak. "I want to braid your hair."

What an actual eff? Braid my hair? That's what he wants to do.

"You're joking, right?" I swivel to catch a glimpse of depth in his eyes that I have never seen before. "Do you even know how to form a braid?"

"I do," he holds my shoulders and turns me around. "Now, watch the movie, and let me braid your hair."

I look over my shoulder to gape at him, but he nudges my face back on the screen.

His fingers sift through my tangled hair as he gathers them together, leaving a soft trail of his fingertips on my skin. I close my eyes and sigh as he parts my hair and starts braiding my loose strands gently, rhythmically.

Somewhere in the middle of this relaxing feel of his soothing touch in my hair, the saddest part of the movie comes up, and I'm sniffling quietly. My Eyes burn, and my nose gets runny as I feel his fingers pause mid-way.

"It's just a movie, V." I can feel the vibration of his voice on my back as I lean on him. I shift against him, resting my chin on his chest, and gaze into his calm eyes.

He brushes away the tears peeling down my cheeks and rests his palm on my face as I mumble, "I'm so happy that we're friends again."

"Me too, V." He tips his head down and places a kiss on top of my head, then stretches back on the couch. The soft rhythm of his heartbeat and the warmth radiating from his body makes my eyelids heavy. And as I lose my senses to sleep, a thousand questions swirl inside my head.

Why can't I stop thinking about his lips touching mine, and why can't I stop myself from wanting more than a touch of fire? I want to burn, and it's toxic for my fragile heart, which still belongs to you, Augustus. This. Is. So. Messed. Up.

06 | This Thing Between Us

In the morning, when I open my eyes, I'm not on the couch, not snuggled up against Adrian's warmth. I'm in my bed, wrapped in my fluffy blanket. The sun is high up in the sky and streaming through the gaps in my window drapes.

As my brain slowly resumes functioning and my braids come undone, a pang of loneliness hits me with the thought that Adrian might've left while I was asleep. I move only my gaze, following the length of my room. The desk looks clean, and the books are on the bookcase beside it.

Did he arrange my room? Thank God! My dirty laundry was in the hamper.

I hear Olivia's faint voice in the hall, but I take my sweet time getting out of bed. I showered and dressed in my yoga pants and a tank top before heading out of my room. The smell of freshly cooked pancakes and coffee fills my nostrils as I roll into the kitchen. When I inch closer, I find Olivia sitting on the island cross-legged in her pajamas with a plate of pancakes and eyes locked at the front. There's an empty mug and a pile of pancakes waiting for me.

"When did you return last night?" I ask her, filling myself with a creamy cup of coffee.

"When you were cuddling with that hunk over there. Why didn't you tell me Adrian's here?" She nudges her head towards the person in question.

"Imagine waking up to that."

I follow her gaze and almost choke on my coffee. Adrian's still here, doing sit-ups in the empty corner of our living room. He never misses an early morning exercise. Watching his biceps bulge and abs crunch with each lift has me transfixed. I take in the neatly folded sheet and a pillow on the couch as I set the coffee on the counter, fixing myself with a plate of pancakes.

He slept on the couch then, after tucking me in my bed.

"Do you think he can pull those off with a hundred pounds on his back?" Liv has a playful glint in her doe eyes and a smirk on her lips.

I fail to look away from Adrian as he switches to the push-up position, elbows bent, face down. He releases low grunts with each dip and rise. My eyes trace a path of those deeply cut pecs slick with sweat and flexing through each of his movements.

"Since you're too dazed off to respond, I might have to try that out with him. I don't think Adrian would refuse me." I hear a sigh from her as she jumps off the island and winks at me, then makes her way toward Adrian. A sudden image of her sitting on Adrian's back flashes in my head, and I beat her to it.

In less than two seconds, I am hovering over Adrian, making him pause on his elbows. He shoots me a surprised look, panting a little with exertion. In another two seconds, his green eyes read what's going on in my mind, and he isn't surprised when I hop on his back, cross-legged, facing his head. Olivia clicks her tongue and shakes her head as I gaze at her over my shoulder. She mouths a "*Fuck you*" before storming towards her room. When I shift my gaze colliding with Adrian's, I feel like a deer caught in headlights as he cocks a brow at me, maintaining his push-up position.

"Good morning to you too, V." He exhales and starts to dip and rise methodically. I place my palms on the ridges of his back as he counts each lift. I relish the feel of his muscles flexing, and the low grunts escaping from his throat add to my pleasure.

"Are you doing fine there with a hundred and twenty pounds on your back?" I chuckle as his body shakes a little after the fifteenth lift. "You can always quit, you know."

"Hundred and twenty pounds or more like ninety?" He presses out a lift with a breathless grunt and collapses with me on his back. "You've lost weight since you stopped eating all that sugar you used to love."

"Is that the reason you added pancakes to my menu?" I push off his back and lay beside him on the floor. I avoid looking into his accusing eyes and brush away the brown hair sticking to his forehead. He lets me until I snap out of my daze. I look from my fingers touching his sweaty hair to his beautiful eyes.

"Blueberry pancakes are your favorite," he inches toward me, pulling on my half-undone braids, the ones he made last night, and undoing them gently. He's crowding me with the musky smell of sweat and his unique scent, which lingered on me until I showered. "At least they were your favorite."

His words tug at my heart. It feels like a lifetime since I ate anything that reminded me of you or the moments we spent together, Augustus. Your existence is as sweet as my sugar rush, and now that you're not here, everything that once tasted sweet leaves a bitter taste on my tongue.

Except, the blueberry pancakes made by Adrian might be the sweetest.

"They're still my favorite, Adri." I stare up at him, getting lost in his forest-green eyes.

"But you still hate sweaty athletes, don't you?" He lifts his head and grins, mischief dancing in his eyes. Before I get the chance to capture his words, he shakes his messy brown hair, and drops of his sweat fall on my face, making me shove him away with a shriek. For the next few minutes, we wrestle like crazy as he runs his sticky skin all over my freshly showered self, and I try my best to defeat his attempts, failing miserably.

Adrian leaves shortly after, turning us into sweaty worn-out kids and making sure I eat the pancakes.

***

I set my laptop on the trunk, cringing at the blaring bass thumping through my bone marrow. Olivia is swaying her hips to the loud and violent lyrics of the rock music. Her long black hair falls on her face as she throws her head to the front and back, following the rhythm of the thrashing music.

She's supposed to help me with the *Multimedia* assignment instead of wrecking my nerves with her insane selection of songs. Sometimes her choice of music and lifestyle reminds me of Daisy, the better version of me, my little sister. I lean back on the couch as my mind drifts back home.

I gaze at my phone on the trunk lying amongst the empty Pizza boxes and cans of coke. My father must have returned from his MRI test about an hour ago, but there's no call or text from my mother. The anxiety has started creeping underneath my skin, expecting all sorts of heartbreaking possibilities. I'm scared to call and check on my dad's test results.

"You're not helping, Vio." The music suddenly turns down, and Olivia glares at me with her hands on her hips. "You're supposed to teach me one of those sensual hip movements they do in the club. We're going to a nightclub after the upcoming soccer game, and Noah has asked me to go dancing with him."

She huffs and walks up to me. "You know I've zero sense of dance forms, especially the sensual ones, and that's the exact kind I want with Noah."

"And you were supposed to help me with my assignment." I roll my eyes, making a place for her legs as she sprawls on the other end of the couch. She leaves the rock music on as it vibrates through the floorboard under my feet. At least, it's turned down to the minimum volume. "Besides, you were acing those moves the other night at the party."

"I was shit-faced." She groans, rubbing her face. "I want to dance with Noah properly, not under the influence of any liquid courage."

"As if you can resist being drunk. You're going to a nightclub, not a church. The smell lingers in the air, and you've zero self-control when it comes to alcohol. I think we've settled that." I laugh at her, momentarily glancing at my phone. *No calls. No texts.*

"Not this time. I'm not ruining my time with Noah this time." She pulls her sweaty hair up in a messy bun and grumbles.

A grin appears on my face as I capture her *caught red-handed* expression. "So, you and Noah are a thing now?"

She grabs a cushion and throws it on my face, followed by her face falling into my lap. "We're not a thing. And I'm afraid Noah thinks I'm gross after I puked all over his shirt last night. I'm not embarrassing myself anymore in front of him."

I play with a strand of her hair falling loose on her face and try to forget the memory of Adrian braiding my hair on the same couch. I can't stop the butterflies waltzing inside my belly that I feel whenever I think about our moments. They're no more like the ones we used to have when we were teenagers. These moments are intense on a level I've never experienced.

"I'm sorry, Vio. I shouldn't have encouraged you to date, Liam." Olivia twists in my lap to look up at me with a soft apologetical smile. "Why do I always have a crush on asshole guys? I wish he gets expelled from the team for his non-consensual behavior towards girls. But I'm happy that his actions brought you and Adrian closer."

"Me too, Liv. I'm happy to have our friendship back." A ghost of a smile appears on my lips as my mind drifts to the friendly kiss we shared. I shouldn't think about that kiss. Erase that moment and move forward before it claws my heart. But the sensation it creates pulls me back at that moment, tingling my skin and accelerating my breaths.

Olivia narrows her brow as I focus my mind back on the present and clear my throat. "You sure about that friendship, Vio? The way you both were tangled up against each other in this exact spot last night tells a different story." She pauses to squeeze my hand and peer into my eyes. "Is it just friendship, though?"

I glare at her ridiculous ways of bulldozing into my chaotic brain and wreaking havoc on my messy heartstrings. "We're friends, Liv, like forever and always."

Olivia shakes her head, shifting her gaze to the ceiling before saying, "This thing between you and Adrian, it's the rarest one. Try not to ruin it anytime soon."

The light thumping of the latest rock number reaches a crescendo, creating a train of confusing thoughts and ideas in my hazed-up mind. I feel overwhelmed with so many emotions, shifting between so many time frames. From past to present and to the future, that's equally uncertain like my feelings.

"This thing between us," I rest my head on the armrest of the couch, releasing an exasperated breath as I feel Adrian's soothing touch embracing me, pushing away all the anxiety from my system. "I will always protect."

***

I'm still thinking about my father's test results when I curl up in my bed late at night. It seems like my mom, and I are trying to avoid the same thing- breaking down in front of my dad. She never speaks about his health condition, and I eliminate it from our conversation when he's around.

I flick through Netflix as a distraction from my ugly thoughts when a single text pops up. When another two follow, I exit the app and open the messages.

Adri: Those dark circles under your eyes, I hate them. They look kind of sad on your happy face.

Adri: I'm always here, V. You don't have to be lonely. We could be sad together.

A small smile forms on my lips as I read his words over and again. Yes, we could be sad together. That's what we always do. We stick by each other.

If that's not worth saving, what is?

The last message is from my mom, which I open with a hand over my thudding heart. The whole universe stands still as I hold my breath and read her text.

Mom: Everything is going to be okay. Your dad is going to be okay, and I'll not lose him. We'll not lose him. You'll see.

I can hear a sob somewhere inside my heart as I send a quick response to my mother.

Me: We'll not lose him, mom.

Then I go back to Adrian's last message and read it.

I've been alone, agonizingly lonely in the solitude of loss and hurt. But I'm growing out of it each day, slowly and gradually. And maybe, instead of talking to the ghost of your memories, Dear Augustus, I need Adrian's comfort, warmth, and togetherness.

07 | Not in Control Anymore

My heart squeezes to death, nails digging into my palm to the point that it may draw blood. It hurts so much, so badly, that my insides constrict, and my eyes feel itchy. But I hold all these emotions inside as my gaze collides with Adrian's right before he places a shot from the center of the box into the bottom left corner of the net, landing that extra point on the scoreboard to win the game.

As the evening sky darkens, we're able to keep buckling down defensively and stifle Costa Rica's potent attacks. When the full-time approaches, they nearly score off a spectacular off-balance shot which our Keeper Noah parries off to seal our win.

Olivia almost jumps out of the bleachers into the track, but I pull her back on the seat.

Some of the tension from my limbs dissipates as Adrian flashes one of his charming, sunshine smiles in my direction before calling his entire team for a group hug. The crowd is already crazy with the cheers of victory, chanting his name, screaming their lungs out, and among them is Charlotte, going an extreme length of wild.

"That was so hot." Olivia squeals in my ear as Noah pulls off his gloves with his teeth and winks in her direction. "God, I might kiss him right now. Do you mind if I leave?"

"Go for it, girl," I mutter, my eyes still searching for his green ones. I was able to pull off my okay face in front of Olivia, or she would be spending the rest of her evening with me instead of going out with Noah, and I don't want her to do that, so I say, "Maybe, try to take his consent first."

We look over to Liam sitting on the bench with a tight jaw and disdain etched on his red face, and we break into a fit of laughter. He didn't get a chance to play in the first home game of the season. As Olivia kisses my cheek and strides off to Noah, my mind goes back to Adrian, the boy who now stands surrounded by his team and coach.

I let myself capture the frowns on his forehead as he sips bottled water and runs a hand through his sweaty brown hair. He looks so young yet authoritative and totally in control of his responsibilities as a captain. A sudden urge to smoothen his frowns and run my hands gently on his tense shoulders forces me to look away from him.

As the crowd in the bleachers starts dispersing, I make my way toward Adrian, who leads his team out of the ground. I'm holding on to a thin thread of breaking down, and the only person who can prevent me walks toward me, with equal desperation, as if he can see through my façade.

Covered in sweat and dirt, he heads right for me, side-stepping the spectators swirling around him. The exertion from scoring three goals in a single game is visible on his face, but that's what serves as a magnetic pull for the girls who appear to be dazzled by him. The headband makes him look drop-dead gorgeous in his jersey and athletic shorts. He has always been this charismatic and insanely breathtaking.

He's just an arm's reach away from providing me my dose of comfort when Charlotte sweeps between us. A knot forms in my stomach as she rises on her tiptoes and places her customary kiss on his cheek. That kiss burns my throat, my eyes, and every inch of my insides. I want to push her away from him, and I'm sure Adrian won't even step in between if I did that. But why would I do that? I'm his friend, and friends shouldn't feel like this if a girl kisses their best friend. I instantly look away and head to the side doors making a hasty exit.

"V!" Adrian's muffled voice echoes through the stomping feet of the crowd and my own heart thudding wildly, but I don't stop until I'm out of the stadium.

I head straight for the washroom and spend the next fifteen minutes inside one of the stalls, letting out all that pain I've held in all this while.

My dad has gone through another test, *MRI,* and *CT scan* for the tumor. My parents hid from me that there was a chance of cancer. If Daisy hadn't called me in the morning crying over how sick dad has been over a month now and how mom cries every night, I would be living in the dark for another month or maybe till it was too late to conceal. I should be there with my family. They need me. Mom, dad, and Daisy they're going through their pain without me. I ball my fists in my hair and let the ugly truth settle in.

I can't lose my father.

Be strong, Violet. Tough girls don't cry. You are Daisy's big sister, your dad's support, and your mom's strength.

Tears wiped and hair finger-combed, I take a deep painful breath and step out of the bathroom stall. I take support of the sink, pressing a fist against my chest as my heart keeps knocking rapidly. A girl with swollen red eyes and flushed cheeks looks back at me through the mirror. Damn! The dark circles around my eyes remind me of Adrian's messages.

Those dark circles under your eyes, I hate them. They look kind of sad on your happy face.

I'm always here, V. You don't have to be lonely. We could be sad together.

I groan and look away as the need to hear his voice crawls back. But I can't give up on pushing those needs away. They can never renew, not when I know they can never mean anything more than a friendly buzz. Straightening my spine, I wash my face and practice my go-to smile before stepping out. I'm halfway through my escape when I get accosted.

"Violet!" Charlotte's shrill voice catches me off guard. Her long blonde hair drops perfectly on her shoulder. She engulfs me with her perfume even from a good one-arm distance. She smells like bubblegum, and if it's so appealing to me, I can only imagine what effect it had on Adrian when she was just an inch away from him. "Why do you look so pale?" she asks.

Charlotte has never once talked to me in three years. But since Adrian and I started having problems in our friendship, she takes on every chance to show off her connection with him.

"I'm good, thanks for asking," I say, still contemplating her nice gesture. She's not checking in on my mental health or my health in general.

She leans in to whisper. "A little bird told me about you and Adrian being friends with benefits, fuck buddies, you know. Of course, it might sting to be his side dish when he chooses me to be his main course. I would've let him go if I were you."

Her sly comment has me clenching my teeth, and the urge to punch her beautiful face gnaws my skin. I know it was doomed to happen. Liam wouldn't just take the punch for me at his house party and not talk shit about me. Others' opinion of me doesn't matter, but that smug smile on Charlotte's face is damn infuriating to let go.

"I never let go of people who are important to me, Charlotte. And Adrian is damn important to me." I give her a warning look before shoving her shoulders out of my proximity. "It doesn't matter what you or the entire college think about our friendship, but my Adri is not a player. He doesn't do the stuff your little bird mentioned. If he chose you, then it will be just you."

She gives me a bored expression and opens her mouth for another comeback, but I don't wait. I'm not going to behave like her. I've nothing to be ashamed of or feel even the slightest bit of embarrassment.

With a deep breath, I swing open the door to the fluorescent-lit hallway, still buzzing with the crowd. I take a nervous glance at the locker rooms, subsiding the need to meet the boy with brown hair and green eyes. Charlotte's words ring in my ear, making me take a beeline to the side exit that leads directly to the parking lot, but I pause to look across me as Olivia throws her head back and laughs at one of Noah's jokes. They look so good together that it makes me crave the same connection, the one I wanted to be with you, Augustus but never had.

I'm so lost in my head that my heart almost lurches out when Adrian sneaks up behind me. I swivel around and look up to meet his grinning self. His smile fades away as instantly as it came and replaces a wary look.

"V," he whispers. We're close, not touching, but I can smell his aftershave and get consumed by the unique scent of his cologne. He draws closer, examining my face, looking through the poker face I've put up the moment I turned around, and he is so close to breaking it down. He's shirtless, his jersey tucked inside his pants, hanging low on his left hip. The outline of his pectoral muscles and the perfect contours of his abdominal muscles makes it almost impossible to step away from him. I gaze at the intense expanse of his neck, and I am still trying to settle my choppy breaths. Then, butterflies start flapping inside my stomach, with a simmering hot feeling that startles me. "What's going on in your crazy little head?"

I lean an inch away from him and brush away the hair falling on my face. I trip backward, stepping away from him and that hot feeling he set inside me. I look over his shoulder at Charlotte as she steps out of the washroom and joins the group of girls. She whispers something to them, all their eyes in our direction, and they all cackle up, not even trying to be subtle.

"Nothing you should be concerned about," I say, looking back at him and swallowing the lump that forms in my throat. "You were on fire tonight, Adri. I'm so proud of you."

"Oh, you are?" He grins, then his palm flattens against my forehead in the gentlest of touches, and he frowns. "You're burning up, V."

"I'm heading back home." I pull his hand away from my forehead, keeping my eyes on him. He looks concerned, lips parted, lashes bobbing as he blinks rapidly at me. Too much. Everything is too much. I need to run away from this while I still have a hold on my emotions. I turn and run towards the exit, rushing past the crowded concourse.

"Wait, V!" Adrian grabs my arm, stopping me. "Don't do that."

"Do what?" I ask, spinning around with a glare.

"Don't step away from me every single time when you need me." The words are hard and desperate, gnawing at my heart.

"I'm sorry, Adri. But what I need is to be alone right now," I snatch my arm away, and he lets me.

In quick strides, he's crowding me. His muscles tense, and my eyes follow the ripples from his chest to the soccer shorts hanging low on his hips. A bunch of red flags waves inside my head, and I squeeze my eyes. "Know that it doesn't matter what they say. I can break each of their faces if they are the reason for your long face, but I'm trying to be a better person. You make me want to be a better me, and that's a goddamn special bond we share."

"I should..." I step backward with my breath stuck in my throat. "I need to go home."

"I guess you're right. You don't even want to share your feelings with me. So fine. Just go home." He shakes his head and releases a dark laugh before jogging away from me. I don't fail to capture the defeated look in his disbelieving green orbs.

I also don't fail to recognize my erratic heartbeat caught in the heat of his eyes.

Oh, God! I'm attracted to my best friend, and the truth is I've been attracted to him before, only this time, it's ten times more intense. It's ten times worse than before because deep in my heart- I still wish for you to come back, Augustus.

Do you even think of me while you're away? The way you kissed me when we parted had to mean something to you, as it means to me. I always believed that living in the memory of the one you love is a choice we make.

Then a look into Adrian's soul-reaching eyes, and I know there are feelings beyond our choices.

What's happening to me? Am I falling for another man?

08 | Is It Too Late to Fix?

I don't know how much time has elapsed since I ran away from my grief. I decided to sleep it off instead. I can feel my skin burning up, which Adrian had mentioned before I pushed him aside. And I do that to him quite often. It amazes me how he still stands by me through every storm in my life. Like right now, as I try wallowing in my pain, emotional and physical, he plans to invade my alone time.

"Leave me alone, Adri," I demand curtly, with gritted teeth, and turn away to face the other side. I can hear his deep sigh as he spends two long seconds leaning against the door jamb of my bedroom, and then it's dead quiet, almost like he isn't there. I squeeze my eyes, praying for him to leave, but soon realize it's too late.

"Not going to happen, V," I hear his stubborn voice, then feel his presence as he stands at the edge of the bed and looks down at me with a determined face. He places an envelope with the symbol of Medlife pharmacy. "Stop behaving like a child, and let me take care of you."

"I don't need anyone, Adri. Just need to rest a bit." He doesn't deserve my rudeness, especially when he ditched his after-match party to be here with me. He clicks his tongue as I push my face on the pillow and hide my face from him. Why does he have to be so caring? He's so stubborn and adorable with that tousled brown hair, slightly disarrayed due to the helmet.

"Can I lie down beside you? I know you need me. And I want to be there for you like you're there for me always." He says, sitting down on the floor near my head, running his cold but soft fingertips on my hair. I'm sure with all the twisting and turning I did from the moment I sprawled on my bed, they must've turned into a pigeon's nest.

I peer up into his dreamy green eyes, which reflect all the stars in the constellation, as I nod my head with a defeated sigh. With my head pounding and my body burning with the possible fever, I feel so tired to dodge the comfort he's offering. I let him scoop me up and lay me gently a foot away to make room for himself beside me. He doesn't pull me into his arms or shift closer to me. We stay on our sides, facing each other, looking into the depths of each other's starry eyes, his more than mine.

We have done this before, many times, for him more than me. That one time on Adrian's fourteenth birthday, when his dad didn't show up at his birthday party, he climbed up my window for the first time. We stared at each other for ten silent seconds before he sprawled on the floor like a fish and stayed like that the whole night. I couldn't sleep in my fluffy warm bed, knowing he was lying on the cold tiles, curled up like a puppy. In the middle of the night, I heard him crying in his sleep.

And in the morning, when he opened his eyes, he bellowed my name in surprise as he found me beside him, lying on my side, looking at him with so much empathy.

"What are you doing here on the floor, V?" He'd asked, turning to face me. His eyes were red with sleep and the crying he did in his slumber. He blinked at me with disbelief and a hint of hope.

"I'm here for you, Adri. I know you're hurt, but I want to share that with you." I replied, curling my fist over my chest to refrain from touching the soft brown hairs that fell on his green, green eyes. I flashed my early morning smile, which he reciprocated instantly, and that was the first time he gave me fluttering butterflies in my stomach.

It wasn't the last time. The last time we stayed beside each other like this was the morning of the Junior Prom when he stood me up for getting stoned with his soccer teammates. I cried the entire night, sleeping in the dress I was supposed to wear. I didn't care if the ruffles of my lavender-colored prom dress would get destroyed. All I cared for was my heart which crumbled every ticking second of the night.

In the morning, when I woke up, I wasn't surprised to come face to face with Adrian lying on my bed beside me. His hair was messy as always, the green of his eyes had lost their tint due to the redness surrounding them, and he was wearing a black tux. The tux served as the ugly reminder of the heartbreaking night of the prom. Before he could coax me into believing any of his excuses for standing me up, I turned to the other side. And that was the last time we slept on the same bed, him facing my *'I'm so done handling your shit'* back. Until now, as we do it once again, only this time it's me hurting, and he's the one there for me.

"Am I going to lose my dad, Adri?" I ask, lowering my eyelashes. They turn wet with sweat that my eyes suddenly decide to perspire. My lips quiver as I try to be strong but fail as he brushes my wet lashes with his soft thumb.

"It's just a test, V," he tucks a strand of my hair behind my ear, his touch so gentle that it hurts. A warm, fuzzy feeling settles inside my heart as he runs mindless circles at the back of my ear, barely touching. "You should talk to your mom. She's worried for you."

I shake my head once, picking at the nail art Olivia did as a peace offering for eating away all the ice cream I kept in our freezer. "Every time I call her, my heart gets stuck in my throat with the possibility of bad news about dad's health. It scares me, Adri."

"Hey, so what if he has cancer-"

"Don't you dare!" I pop up as if someone zapped me with naked electric wires.

One of my hands flies to his chest, grabbing a fistful of his shirt as I yank it with gnashing teeth. His mouth opens for a cry, but he closes it, looking into my eyes with a glint of surprise, and then he swallows harshly, his Adam's apple bobbing. I was so clueless when I jumped on top of him, my hands bunched up against his chest, but now I realize I'm just in my short cotton shorts and a baggy shirt. *Kill me.* I can feel his erratic heartbeat against my palm as I ease them on his shirt, and I don't miss how his hands clamp around my waist, preventing me from sliding any further downtown, which I'm sure I can feel swelling with excitement.

A particular scene from one of many romance novels adorning my bookshelf pops up in my head. The mere picture of me doing that with Adrian as his sparkling green eyes look into mine has me hyperventilating, and I'm ready to burst into flames, both from fever and the heat of his taut muscles underneath me.

Oh, holy mother, I want to stay like this, but I can't. I shouldn't.

"Don't...don't say that again, okay," I mumble in a shaky voice, relaxing away from his body.

"Okay," he chokes. He doesn't give me a chance to say anything else as he slides away from the bed, brushing a hand through his hair. The door flies open, and his back faces me as he says, "I'll get something for you to eat. You need to take your meds."

I nod as if he's looking at me. Nervous, I slowly inhale, placing a fist against my thudding heart, and exhale, repeating it again and again, but every time, it's the smell of his aftershave and his earthly scent that keeps hazing my mind.

Such. A. Mess.

He returns as quickly as he left, not giving me enough moments to bargain with the unfamiliar feelings surrounding me.

"No, I don't feel like eating, not now."

But my words have zero persuasion on him, and he hands me a bowl of warm soup from the Thai restaurant across the street. He gives me a spoon as I prop myself against the headboard. He pretends to behave, unaware of the tension that still lingers around us, and I pretend not to care either. Behind these nervous smiles are waltzing hearts, I'm sure of mine, his - not so much.

After a few mouthfuls, I turn to face Adrian, who has a lazy grin as he watches me eat, resting his weight on his elbows.

"How do you know the passcode of my apartment?" I ask.

"I saw you enter it last time I came here. Is that a problem?" His expression doesn't change as he reaches to wipe away the corner of my lips, his eyes darken, and I curse my clumsy self for letting the food drip down my chin. I shake my head, looking down, feeling a little dehydrated all of a sudden. "Thought so. Now finish the soup. You haven't eaten all day."

"How do you know that?" I ask, gulping down the rest of the content in the bowl and smacking my lips to savor the mouth-watering taste of Thai cuisine. His eyes follow my movements.

"I just figured, and I have something else for you. Wait here." Adrian clears his throat, taking the empty bowl from my hand and carrying them out to the kitchen. I stay on the bed, watching him stride into the hall. He emerges, hiding something behind his back and throwing me one of his *'I got you a surprise'* grins.

I tilt my head, attempting to push away my untamable hair from my face. "It can't be worse than the soup. You know, I hate soup."

He settles back on the bed beside me, helps me tame those untangled strands, and then touches my nose teasingly. "Close your eyes for a second."

My frown deepens, but I close my eyes nonetheless, getting impatient for whatever he has for me. He gently grabs my hand and places a soft fabric on my palm. The time remains suspended as I open my eyes and look down at what he just handed me. I breathe once and then some more. He did not just give me his soccer jersey, the one he wore today. It has his name and #1 painted on the back. My mouth opens to say something, but I don't and bunch the soft material in my hand.

"What's wrong?" He asks, wetting his pink lips. It indicates he is dying of nervousness.

"Shouldn't you be giving this to Charlotte?" My voice is sharper than I intend it to be. My heart starts beating against my chest, waiting for his response.

"Charlotte? No. I shouldn't be giving it to anyone but you." He stretches on the bed, places his hands underneath his head, and closes his eyes. "I want you to wear it when you come for the home game next weekend and the next. Every fucking time, I want my best friend to wear it, and Charlotte isn't the one. You are."

I'm lit from the inside, beaming like a lovesick fangirl. It's good that Adrian has his eyes closed, else he would freak out from my reaction. I quickly recover and fold the jersey, breathing his faint scent on the fabric. It's too irresistible. But before I inhale my fill, he snatches it from my hand.

"I know, it's smelly and gross. Sorry, I didn't get time to wash it." He blinks slowly and scrunches his nose, smelling himself on the jersey.

I can't stop the low rumbling laugh that emerges due to the adorable look on his face. "Give it back. It's mine now. I will wash and iron it later."

He hands it back to me and stays propped on his elbows as I walk toward my dresser. I place the jersey with the rest of my clothes, shaking my head to remind myself to ignore all the butterflies going crazy inside my tummy.

When I return to the bed, he's holding the medicine and a glass of water. "Time for the medicine."

I hesitate at first, but then he forces me to take them. As I gulp down the meds, his fingertips sift through my loose strands, his eyes following the way my untamed hair rebels with his fingers and fall back on my face. I remind myself again he's not the one

I want, not the way I should've wanted you and you alone, Augustus.

"I think I'll have to braid them again. Your hair is as wild as you are." He grumbles, tugging at my hair gently. But the action makes my eyes lock with his, and for a sinful second, I wish he would hold them a little firmly. I wish I had done the same, letting my fingers dive into his messy brown hair. I remember the fiery feel of his lips, and I want them back on mine. This time, I want them to fuse with mine. I need a deep thunderous kiss or maybe a little breathless one. But I shouldn't wish for that one kiss. Not with him. Never with my best friend. Adrian Hayes, not in this lifetime.

I smile and hand him the glass back, which he finishes, then places it on the nightstand.

"So, what should we do next?" I hop on the mattress, my legs hanging from the edge. I flatten my palms on the bed behind me and lean back. "Are you up for zombies?"

He snorts, bends down, then holds my legs, forcing me to shift further up. "Do I have a choice?"

"None."

He has no choice but to recline beside me. We lean back on the headboard with pillows surrounding us and play the latest season of Walking Dead on my laptop. As I shiver, feeling a lot more feverish than before, he drapes a blanket over my body. His fingertips graze my skin lightly, and our gazes meet, sending sparks of electricity through my veins. Adrian's whiskey-scented lips, rain-drenched quivering lips, and now anticipation-painted lips, I want to feel them all, but I don't.

"You know what I said about your dad," he breathes quietly. "What I wanted to say was - so what, if your dad has cancer tests that don't specifically mean he has cancer."

I curse myself mentally for not letting him complete his words earlier. Even more, when he looks pained. I give his hand a light squeeze and smile gently. "I'm sorry, Adri. I know how much he means to you. I also know how much of an insensitive bitch I am."

His green eyes lock with mine, pinning me with a warning look. " You're not. Don't ever say that about yourself, okay," he says sharply. "You're not insensitive." He adds slowly, touching my chin, nudging it toward the laptop screen where Rick rips through a swarm of walkers like nothing. Then he straightens his long legs, crossing them at the ankles, and leans back against the headboard. I mirror his pose, letting my body relax, and I don't miss the comfort that follows as our shoulders brush. I crane my neck to look at him as he dives his warm fingers through my hair, massaging my scalp with a lazy smile decorating his lips.

He looks so much like my tranquilizer, dosage a bit higher. My eyelids feel heavy, and I snuggle up little by little to his side, breathing in his warmth and comfort, wishing it to last forever, never to let go but stay.

I must have drifted off. When I open my eyes, I feel warm and sweaty. Maybe it's due to my fever going down, but it doesn't take long to know the real reason. At some point, Adrian snuggled up behind me, his warm body pressed firmly against my back, and our legs tangled together. I can hear the rain splatter against the windowpane in the background, the laptop screen black. It isn't the first time we are cuddling, although it feels entirely different this time.

Adrian's labored breaths tickle my neck and turn my breathing erratic and shallow. The closeness of our bodies has me flush, setting me on fire as his fingertips run gingerly across my covered thigh. I can feel him hard against me. The soft material of the shorts I'm wearing does nothing to ease out the feel of his touch. I squirm unknowingly as his fingers trail a path upward, following the curve of my hip, and hold it firmly until I'm still in his hold again.

I hold my breathing for a few seconds as he ghosts his touch along my arm, running along its length, then feathers his fingers over mine, and I feel so far gone in the electrifying effect of his caresses that I lace my fingers with his. The impulsive, wild Violet wants to let go and lose herself in this moment, following the adventure at hand. But Violet, who feels too much and waits for the one she chose, dreads his touch. I know it won't last once that part of me wins and Adrian regains consciousness.

So, I lay in his arms, waiting for either of them to happen. The warmth of his body seeps through each of my veins, making me hotter with every passing second. And the moment he curls his fingers tightly over mine, releasing ragged hot breaths against my ear, murmuring my name, I explode with a muffled moan. He unscrews his fingers from mine almost instantly, and his breathing stops.

"Violet!" He breathes my full name for the first time with so much vulnerability in his voice. But I don't respond. I close my eyes firmly and pretend I feel nothing. He yanks himself away from my body and turns to the other side of the bed, making us poles apart. His breathing remains rapid even after we're not touching, and I'm on fire even though he's at the other end of the bed.

I crane my neck once my heartbeat normalizes and watch his back tighten with the tension. Something just happened between us, something that wasn't supposed to happen, but it did anyway.

Is it too late to fix this? Or do we even want to fix it? I'm sure I can never undo what happened and certainly can't get it out of my head, either. If I'm honest with myself, I want to live this sinful moment again.

Will you hate me, Augustus, if I can never let go of this feeling?

09 | Not A Mistake

The fallout is inevitable. When you want something so badly that you surpass all logics or mental warnings, it's doomed to get snatched away from you the moment you become defenseless.

Ever since our cuddle has gone out of line, Adrian has been avoiding me. Maybe we both are avoiding each other. He left Sunday morning before I woke up, leaving freshly brewed coffee and pancakes on the kitchen island. He stuck a sticky note on the fridge with a smile.

Take your meds on time. I have kept blueberry ice cream in the freezer. Eat it after your fever comes down. :)

There was no mention of the night before, which was good, but it still stung when he ignored it as if it was nothing. He didn't forget it, though. Not when I changed direction every time we crossed paths. Not when the entire soccer team came to the Brew Story, and he chose a far-end corner, away from the counter where our eyes could meet. He didn't even come to place his order. Of course, that would mean facing me, facing the mistake for which we both are equally guilty.

As the week passes, I realize how badly we have fucked up. How can we work through this if we can't look each other in the eyes? Somehow, it's worse this time. It wasn't just a brush of lips, but we crossed some lines. Above all, it's the first time I have experienced something this wild.

I might be immature and inexperienced, but I'm not clueless. Not in my twenties. I do have some idea of why Adrian's mere presence around me ignites an inextinguishable fire within me. No part of him touches me, but he doesn't have to. His green possessive eyes are enough to drive my pulse crazy, and God forbid he does- my insides thrum with mindless anticipation. But we are still best friends. Friends don't feel this way for each other. It is so wrong, and I'm not sure how to make it right.

I bite my lip to pull myself out of my reverie and move back to cleaning the counter, using a towel to wipe up coffee spills.

"You fight with him again?" Andrea asks, helping me clean up the counter before heading over to flip the sign on the door.

I pull off my work apron, place it back on the rack, and turn to pin my co-worker with a *what are you talking about* look. Andrea has a lazy smile across her pink-tinted lips as she shakes her head and continues to arrange the disarrayed chairs. She's a year junior, but we've bonded well over our shifts in the café. Andrea has a rare superpower to know what's going on in people's minds. Crazy as it sounds, she's correct most of the time.

"You know I don't possess the same mind-reading talent as you," I roll my eyes, continuing to arrange the counter.

"Adrian," she leans against the doorframe of the back room. "You guys are dodging each other. And taking subtle glances when the other one isn't watching. To top it off, you are missing your signature smile."

I snort, swinging the towel over my shoulder and turning around. "Sorry for having a bad day. And no, it has nothing to do with Adri."

"Yeah, you can keep saying that, but I know the look."

I lift my brows in question, then shake my head. "Can you stop invading everyone's thoughts for once? It's not cute anymore. You're creeping me out."

She smiled, knotting her black curls into a high bun. "So, are you going to tell me now what's going on between you and your sexy-ass best friend?"

I heave a deep sigh, looking at her with a knowing look. I can't stop the way my lips lift as I think about Adrian's brown, messy hair and how they feel soft under my fingertips. My fingers still remember the feel of his fingers and how well they lace together with mine. His ocean eyes, I miss looking deep into them. *God!* I need to sort our distance.

"Tell me you're not thinking about him right now?" Andrea laughs. Her warm, playful voice pulls me out of my thoughts.

I stare at her and nod softly, regretting immediately as her jaw drops open. "So, it is what I thought."

"What exactly are your thoughts? Please enlighten me." I groan, pausing midway to stock the coffee beans. I give her a warning look as she gestures to me to continue filling the bean hopper.

"You're trying to tame your feelings towards him. Maybe, you'll win, or maybe your feelings will betray you. Either way, you can't stop yourself from seeking something your heart wants. The heart wants what it wants." She sighs, leaning on her palms. "Avoiding each other may not be the wisest way to deal with your feelings."

Adrian's warm breath against my ear and his velvety touch haven't left me alone for a minute. "There's no such feelings between us. My heart still belongs to Augustus. I don't think I can ever feel the way I feel for him, but he isn't here."

Andrea hops on the counter, crosses her legs at the ankles, then nods. "You still wait for him?"

I didn't think I could cry any more tears for you, Augustus, but here I am, blinking them away. "A part of me wants to let him go, but I can't. Not when there's even one percent chance of us reuniting." I sniffle, brushing away the drops of tears making their way down my cheeks. "It's breaking me, this continuous whirlwind of emotions. My dad's sick, and Adri is the only person who makes me forget all this pain and anxiety."

A warm smile spreads on her face as she stops my trembling fingers on the countertop and pulls me into a bear hug. I let her calm fruity scent ease my wrecking nerves as she rubs my back.

"So, stop pushing away the only anchor you've got."

She's right. That's how Adrian feels.

He's the anchor to my wrecked soul.

***

There's this constant heartbreak that surrounds me every day. I have no clue how to get rid of it. Sometimes it's bearable, almost there but not quite deep, and sometimes it walks with me like my shadow. I look in the mirror every morning, come face to face with the ghost of my free-spirited self, and dress ready to profess, to pretend that everything's fine, that I'm fine. Then tilt my head in question. When will everything be okay? When will I be okay?

My plans have always been simple: Graduate from college, move back to *Winsbay*, to join my father's law firm. And somewhere along the line - publish a novel. I know it's not something extraordinary, but I never wanted it to be one.

"What about your masters?" Adrian would say, and I might take a few extra seconds to reconsider. But with my father's health condition, it doesn't matter.

There will always be something or the other, something to lose, something at stake. The question is- what am I willing to let go? I'm sure it can never be the people I love.

And right at this moment, as I wait for Professor Bradshaw to finish the lecture, my mind is infused with Adrian and how he has constantly been avoiding interactions with me. Although, he talks to my mom every day. I shouldn't be jealous of my mom, but I'm very anxious. Like now as I see his brown hair and the pen tucked behind his ear from two desks away.

He was already in class when I entered, and for the briefest second, our gazes met. I didn't miss the tiredness in those green eyes, missing their notorious glint. He has been spending more time in his soccer practice than usual, and it has started showing up on his face. For a few fleeting seconds, I stood by the stairs as students passed me, and I hesitated, thinking whether to take my usual seat beside him or move to the empty ones behind him. And while we kept staring into each other's eyes, mine unsure, his full of anticipation, Charlotte snatched my place.

My fingers latched tightly around the laptop in my hand, and my jaw tightened as she kissed his cheeks. All the while, his attention never shifted from me. It hurt. It hurt too much to look at her taking my place, but I gulped down the bile forming in my throat. As a few students bumped into my back, I realized how stupid I looked standing still at the entrance and collapsed at the next empty seat that caught my eye.

My nerves are still on fire as I exhale the possessiveness coursing through my veins by looking at the girl with blonde hair sitting in my place with my best friend, Adri. She leans her head towards his ear and whispers whatever the hell she needs to when we are practically in the middle of an important lecture.

As Professor Bradshaw turns towards the board, Charlotte grabs the opportunity to run her lean fingers with raging red, long nails on Adrian's hair, making me clench my fists on my lap and close my eyes. I have felt like this before, and it goes back to my high school days. Nothing has changed, Adrian is making me feel like that once again, and I'm handing him the power to do that. And you weren't there then, Augustus, just like you aren't here now.

I dread every passing second for the rest of the class until the lecture ends. I grab my bag, putting away my things fast as I hear shuffling from the desks in front of me. Before Adrian can reach my seat, I'm out of the class and into the hallway, away from him. My heart tugs to have a conversation with him. But I know with the current state of my heart - I'll mess it up anyway.

***

After spending the entire lunch break inside the library, mentally preparing myself and rehearsing all my lines, I finally put my foot down. It takes me almost fifteen minutes to figure out that he has been back to the soccer field. *Oh boy!* His untimely extensive workout means he's pissed, and probably I'm one of the reasons.

I don't see him on the grounds, and the locker room is the only place left in the athletic building where I can find him. When I walk down the hallway to the locker room, I spot a few soccer players heading out with their bags over their shoulders, but none of them have those sparkling green eyes, the ones I'm looking for.

I hesitate for a second, working on my nerves before I push the door open and appreciate God internally for the lack of audience inside. My eyes sweep across the rows of lockers and benches, rubbing my forehead for being crazy enough to be inside the boys changing room. I can hear the shower running for a few seconds before it's shut off. I shift from one foot to another and contemplate waiting for whoever is about to come out or rush outside. What if it's not Adrian? It would be hell awkward to explain why I'm here. But that doesn't seem as challenging as the possibility that the person might be Adrian. My heartbeat turns erratic, and I'm about to chicken out, but I stay glued to the spot when he walks out of the corner.

I yelp as my eyes lock with his green ones and then travel down the expanse of his sculpted body, freshly showered. I swallow a lump in my throat as I watch water droplets trickling down his damp hair to his neck, pausing over one nipple before it continues under the bulge of his pectorals. A white towel is wrapped low around his waist, and I gawk shamelessly, tracing the path those droplets follow before they finally disappear in the trail of a dark line of hair running down his stomach. It ruins all the prep I did for this moment because I become speechless. He seems to have the same effect as me. At least I've got my clothes on.

"V?" Adrian's voice makes me look back into his eyes. He raises his brow in question, and when I don't speak for a long time, he grabs a fresh towel from the stand. "Why are you here, V?"

I gulp as my throat suddenly feels dry, and no words leave my lips. Adrian sighs. He throws the towel in his hand on the bench and takes a few steps closer to me. With each of his forward steps, I take one back until my back hits the locker, and I wish it swallows me. It doesn't. And I'm done for - once he is close enough to let me get consumed in the smell of his aftershave and bathing gel.

"You shouldn't be here," he says, pausing a foot away from me. His eyes look tired and full of worry as he snaps towards the door. "It's the boys' locker room, for god's sake."

"I-" I choke, then place a hand over my heart to ease my irregular breathing. "I needed to talk to you, and what does it matter if it's the boys' locker room?"

"It does matter," his jaw locks, and now I'm successful in pissing him off again. So much for having a decent conversation. He takes another step closer to me and leans towards my ear, his breath hot against my skin as he breathes, "Because I wouldn't want you looking at any other guy the way you just looked at me."

"What way?" My jaw drops on a stalled breath. He tips his cold finger under my chin and closes my mouth.

"The way you shouldn't look at your friend. However, I don't blame you for that. I know it's hard to resist me." A low laugh rumbles inside his throat, and I shove at his shoulder with a huff. He doesn't budge from his position. Instead, he touches my chin and turns my face to the side. He then traces the drops of sweat on the corner of my face. "Look, you're already sweating."

"Don't do that," I look him in the eyes, not letting his lazy grin distract me.

"Do what?" He asks, running a hand through his damp hair while leaning away. I subside the urge to do it myself.

"Behave like an obnoxious prick," I scoff at him. I take a deep breath, adjust to his bare torso, and steel my spine. "I'm here to talk."

"I'm here to change, and I can do that with you watching." He braces a hand on the locker beside my head and inconspicuously adjusts the towel around his waist. "Also, you're leaning on my locker."

"I'm not leaving unless we finish talking," I tip my head up to glare at him, then fold my arms across my chest. He can't avoid conversation this time. I'm done feeling awkward around each other because of some stupid hormonal disbalance. That's what it was, a lapse in judgment. We're two sexually active young individuals, and it's normal if some lines get blurred while we sleep on the same bed. I rest my head back on the locker and smile, throwing a challenging look at him.

He shakes his head and scowls at me with wet, full soft lips. "Okay, let's talk, but then you'll leave before the guys from the track team are back here."

Trying not to get distracted by the flexes of his muscled chest, I chew the corner of my thumb and start in a rushed breath. "I - Whatever happened the other day- night, I don't want that to come between our friendship. You probably don't care, but I do. I can't lose you because of my stupid impulse. The truth is, I hate not being able to look you in the eyes without getting reminders of the mistake, the mistake I'm equally guilty of. I'm so sorry, Adri." I finally release a breath.

"Shh," he places a finger on my lips, stopping me. His eyes look deep into my eyes, hurt radiating from them. "Don't say that. Don't ever say sorry. That's the reason I didn't want to confront it."

"What? Me owning my mistake?" I laugh, my voice breaking.

He runs a hand through his tousled hair before he laughs, dark, "No, you calling it a mistake as if you didn't feel a thing."

My breath hitches as his words electrify every cell in my body. "What?"

He curses, closes his eyes, then releases a staggered breath. "Fine! Let's call it a mistake then and forget that it ever happened. In that case, I'm sorry too for making you writhe with pleasure in my arms, for making you moan, and for making you-"

"Adri!" I growl, gritting my teeth and hitting his chest. "If you are going to behave like an asshole, then we are done talking. God! I hate you so much." I step away from his locker and rush for the exit, swiping the strands of hair falling on my face.

I get to hardly cross two lockers when a hand grabs my arm, making me stop and turn towards two pleading green eyes. "We're not done talking. You can hate me all you want, but I will never call any of our moments a mistake. You've done that before and are doing it now. I said this before, and I'm saying it now- what I felt was not wrong. I've never felt anything as right as that."

I struggle to breathe, glaring at him but breaking down internally. My heart thrums and wants to get embraced in his comfort, not the tension he's offering. "I miss you, Adri. I need you now more than ever and all these confusing emotions. They're killing me. They're breaking us apart, and I don't- I can't lose you."

"Come here," he says softly, pulling me toward himself. Then gently brushes away the wet trail from my cheeks. He holds my nape, joining our foreheads, and breathes hotly against my skin. "I missed you too, V, fucking every single day. Couldn't even sleep, knowing that you might be hurting."

"I don't want to stop being friends," I say, tears bubbling.

"Then let's not avoid each other, okay," he mumbles, pinching the collar of my shirt that hung off my shoulder and sliding it back. "Although, I do have to confess."

The playful tug on his lips tells me he's ready to pull us out of the tension surrounding us.

"Confess." A laugh escapes me.

"It was all your mistake. You're the only one guilty here," Adrian whispers in my ear while walking me backward, holding onto my shoulders. "You've turned into a walking sin. It's hard to resist someone as potent as you. It was my test of self-control, and I failed because of you, my stubborn little sinner."

One moment Adrian's scent is everywhere, clouding my senses, soothing my aching heart, and his words blurring my vision, and in the next moment, he nudges me outside the locker room with a soft caress of his whiskers over my neck. "Wait for me after the classes. I know you skipped your lunch, and we need to fix your hunger first."

I flatten my trembling palm over my rumbling heart and turn back. The door closes after, but I can feel Adrian's presence on the other side.

He has unleashed something new in me, and I'm sure it's soul-deep.

10 | The Remnant of Heartbreak

I spot Adrian's black Harley as I trail into the college parking lot. Had I known I was up for another bike ride with Adrian, I would've left my convertible back home. But thanks to Olivia. She gladly took my cooper home. So, here, I lean against the black beast reminiscing each of Adrian's words on a loop.

My little sinner.

A shiver runs down my spine as I recall his heated whisper and the light feathery feel of his whiskers over my neck. So, this is the reason Charlotte can't keep her hands to herself. Because when Adrian is around you with all that masculine charm and woodsy scent, it's next to impossible not to crave more of his closeness.

I'm still lost in my thoughts when I feel his hot breath against the back of my neck. My smile bites into my cheeks as Adrian sneaks up behind me and blows hot air into my hair. When I spin around to look at his face- he walks over to my front. He traps me against the bike, placing his hands on both sides of my waist. His arms slide close to mine, and my skin prickles as the tiny hairs rising on our skin meet in the gentlest of touches.

"You've no idea how sexy you look leaning against my bike," he grins. His ocean-green eyes have regained their mischievous glint. He looks so adorable with his windblown brown hair that I brush my fingers through them, trying to get them away from his forehead. His Adam's apple bobs as he swallows and continues, "Now I can say it was a worthy investment. Are you up for the ride?"

"Do you say these cheesy words to all the girls you offer a ride to?" I laugh, pulling my hand away from his hair, but he holds my wrist. His thumb brushes over my veins, and then he lets go.

"What girls?" He says with wrinkled brows while he unlocks the helmets, handing one to me. I adjust it on my head but struggle with the strap under my chin as he sets his helmet on and angles his neck to watch me. "You're the only girl I offer bike rides on my Harley. Other girls, they're certainly more interested in riding m-"

"Adri! That's so fucking gross," I clamp my hand over his grinning lips, letting go instantly as his soft lips touch the inside of my palm. I don't miss the itching pain that hits my heart with the mere picture of him with the girls swooning over him. "I might lose my appetite if you don't stop talking about your girls."

"You started it, no?" He brushes my fingers away, buckles the strap swiftly, then gives it a little tug, making me yelp in surprise. I slap his hands away and push his chest. He places a hand to his heart, releases a groan, and swings a leg over the bike.

"Hop on, my little sinner." He looks over his shoulder as I hook my thighs around his narrow waist, placing a hand on the thick bulge of his shoulder muscles. Adrian is wearing a black leather jacket over the black crew neck t-shirt that highlights every contour of his muscles beneath tight jeans. He slides his hands back, molding his fingers around my jeans-clad thighs, and pulls me closer to his body. I'm still processing his bold moves while he does the same with my arms and guides them around his waist. "Let's go. I'm fucking starved."

He laughs and throttles the motorcycle, making me fall forward toward his body. The way his body heat works against mine, I curl my fingers nervously around him as he arrows the bike at a devilish speed. But I don't close my eyes or shudder under the impact of whips of cold evening air through my hair and the ear-deafening purr of the revving engine. At this moment, I realize that nothing feels more amazing than putting myself in the safety of his hands.

The smell of freshly baked bread and cupcakes tickles my nostrils as he pulls into the parking lot of *Molly's Bakery*. Suddenly I'm hyper-aware of the surroundings. The old brick building with cobblestone sidewalks and the buzz of the diverse population takes me back to our town. The place looks exactly like *Smoothie Shack* back in *Winsbay*. *Smoothie Shack*, where I went on our first date, Augustus, where you worked, where I spent endless evenings watching you and being around you. My fingers fist Adrian's t-shirt tightly as a similar pain washes over me, and I bury my head at his back. "Can we go somewhere else, please?"

"V, do you trust me?" He places his palm over my hand where I'm fisting his t-shirt, and his touch is enough to ease the pain to a bearable ache. He shuts off the engine and twists in my hold to meet my eyes. "I want to serve your sweet tooth for once. Will you let me?"

How can I deny such a sweet request? Not when those soft green eyes look at me with so much adoration and pleadings. So, even though my heart squeezes with the remnant of heartbreak, I nod at him with a forced smile. He places a feathery kiss on my cheek, soothing my aching heart.

And we slide off the bike and lace our fingers together while heading toward the bakery. But I know you'll always waltz in the empty expanse of my heart like a sad melody, and I can never let you go, not in this lifetime, Augustus.

Unspoken tension lingers around us as we cover the distance between the parking and the entrance. Adrian holds the door, nudging me into the cutest bakery I have ever seen. The smell of sweet confectioneries, chocolate, and cinnamon, makes me ignore all the other small details of the place. My mouth waters as my eyes capture the rows of cupcakes, donuts, and my all-time favorite brownies. I'm suddenly famished. My stomach curdles, and Adrian flashes a crooked smile before taking the seat across from me.

"I'm open to your previous request," he says, tapping his fingers on the table. One of his arms drapes along the back of the couch, a sly smirk twitching through his full lips. He knows I'm now desperate for food. The look on his face confirms that. "If you still wish to go somewhere else-"

"No, stop it. I'm hungry," I say, bunching and tossing a napkin. Adrian catches it before it hits his grinning face. "Some obnoxious prick you are, Adrian Hayes."

"What can I say? You bring out the best in me, sinner," he says before swaggering backward towards the counter, waving the menu in his hand. "Since you asked me nicely, I'm gonna feed your hungry belly."

I chuckle, air flicking him, and break into full throttle laugh as he imitates a wince, rubbing his forehead, then bumps straight on the flower decoration. It's probably the first time in days I've laughed so much that my eyes start watering.

Later, after I've satisfied my year's worth of sweet cravings with all the crepes, cupcakes, waffles, and Molly's signature Berry Blast Smoothie, we fall into an uncomfortable silence. It shows there's something in both of our minds.

"Did you quit eating sweets because of him?" Adrian's voice shatters the silence between us. "Does it remind you of him?"

I purse my lips, then avoid looking into his eyes and eye the empty smoothie glass, the remnant of the contents sticking to its sides. "Yeah, it pretty much does." I notice his knuckles turn white as he holds his glass, and when I look up, I find him staring at me with a scowl on his lips.

"You still wait for him, don't you?" His jaw tightens, and I see the possessiveness dancing in those emerald eyes. "Is there anything that doesn't remind you of Goldilocks?"

"Adri, what-" I start, but my throat dries off because the truth is you, Augustus, is always a constant reminder of a deep feeling once I lived so freely.

"Forget it, don't answer that. I already know your answer," Adrian rubs his forehead, and I can see how he gnashes his teeth while swiping the card to pay the bill. "It's too late, V. Let's head back." He stands, then runs his trembling fingers through his hair before charging out of the bakery. It shows he's holding on to a fine thread of self-control and makes me realize how utterly infuriating my choice seems to him. But the why part of his reaction tips me off my balance as it finally dawns upon me that he has feelings for me, more than a friend kind of feeling.

"Adri, wait!" I chase after him, my voice trembling as I follow him to his bike. "I don't understand. Do you-" I begin, but he spins me around, trapping me against his bike a second time in a day. His scent is so raw, and his eyes, blazing greens of hidden emotions, make my knees weak.

"The only thing you need to understand is that it hurts when I see you're hurting for someone who might as well be scoring some hot chick while you're waiting for him like Juliet because I'm sure he isn't your Romeo. Now do me a favor and don't ask me how I feel. You'll probably never understand." The words grit through his perfect set of teeth, his hot desperate breaths warm my face, and the rage radiating through him seizes my heart.

He steps away from me, then sighs, closing his eyes, and when they look at me, I wonder what they see in them. I open my mouth to say something, but my tongue remains tied as he shrugs off his jacket and drapes it around me.

As we drive back, with me plastered against the warmth of his back and wrapped in his scent, I'm not sure who is the reason for this sweet ache in my heart.

11 | Feelings You Have for Me

Sometimes all you need to know is that there is this person, no matter what, who stands by you, not only when you're in need, but always. And I'm afraid I might lose that person. I need to make amends before it's too late and the crack becomes irreparable.

Olivia comes home to find me with a bucket of blueberry ice cream on the couch. *One Day* runs in the background, and the only light in our living room comes from the TV screen.

She doesn't freak out. Instead, she picks up a spoon from the cabinet, sits beside me, and starts eating the almost-melted ice cream from my bucket until it's empty. Then we sit beside each other for as long as I take to recollect my hazing mind.

Olivia plays with my single hoop earring as I place my head on her lap, and she waits for me to talk. I'm wearing Adrian's jacket, and his words are still ringing in my ears like an inner monologue running on replay.

"I think Adri has feelings for me," I finally break the silence. My fingers play with the zipper of the jacket.

She looks down at me with her lips parted. "All this suspense for that. I thought Adrian proposed to you, and you said no."

I sit up, instantly glaring at her. "It's not funny, Liv. Why would you say something like that?"

"Yeah, you're right. It's not funny, Adrian's your best friend. You don't feel anything for him. Your heart still belongs to Augustus." She skates her tongue over her teeth and pulls my head back on her lap. "I get all these. So, what's the big deal here if Adrian has feelings for you? He cares for you, V."

"You don't understand, Liv. If he has feelings for me, and if it's more than what friends feel for each other, then it's not going to end well." I sigh, looking at the white-washed ceiling.

We remain silent for a long time as her fingers ease some of the tension from my scalp. I close my eyes for a brief moment. If I end up hurting Adrian, it will break my heart. I have to fix everything while I still have time. And there's this slightest possibility that I'm wrong about his feelings toward me. Either way, I have to talk him out of it. My heart starts thumping inside my chest.

"You should talk to him before it's too late. Tell him you don't feel the same way and will probably never feel the same." She leans her head back and relaxes her shoulder.

"Can I do that without hurting him?" I gnaw on my bottom lip. My fingers feel cold, and my chest caves.

"It's the only way," Olivia shrugs, her eyes focused on the screen instead of me. "Since you don't have feelings for him, it shouldn't be a problem, or do you?"

I can't lose my best friend because of my selfish emotions. I can never be more than friends with him, not when I can't give my heart to him.

"Vio?"

"Huh," I snap out of my trance and find her looking at me with raised brows.

"You don't have feelings for Adrian, right?"

"No, I don't," I say, closing my eyes as the words knot my stomach.

"Well, that sounded different in my mind, but if that's the truth, then I'm with you." She squeezes my shoulder reassuringly, and I don't miss the disbelief in her eyes. She thinks I'm lying to her and myself.

Am I lying to myself?

After a thoughtful minute, Olivia says, "Tell him not to be sad about it. I'm willing to date him instead of Noah any day."

I push off her lap and toss a pillow at her when a message pops up on her phone. It's from Noah.

She purses her lips as I cross my arms and flash a grin.

"Okay, don't say that when Noah is around." She laughs, and that earns her a flick on the forehead.

***

I'm carrying his leather jacket in one hand and Italian takeout in the other as I jog down the street. The crisp evening air and the blaring sound of the traffic follow me with every step closer to Adrian's apartment. I haven't been to his new apartment, which he shares with Noah. So, I'm excited to see his new place for the first time.

But that excitement is minuscule compared to the anxiety of what I'm about to tell him. We're best friends forever. I still believe we can put all these complicated feelings aside and enjoy our time together. I walk down the narrow hallway and hesitate before ringing the doorbell. I can hear the faint sound of music and laughter through the door.

After the third ring, the door opens, and a red-eyed Noah looks at me as if he has seen a ghost. He hides the red cup behind his back and runs a hand through his hair. I have only seen him sober, so his drunk self catches me by surprise.

"Hey, Violet." He says, giving me a half-smile as I glance at the crowded room over his shoulder. I can spot a few guys from the soccer team.

"Hey, Noah," the Smell of weed and alcohol lingers in the air around us. "Looks like you guys are having a party."

"Yeah, it's just the guys from the soccer team. Last-minute plan, you know." He replies hurriedly, and just as I'm convinced, a petite girl comes beside him with a cup. She throws herself to his side, holding his bicep for support while giggling. Olivia would rip this girl's arms off her shoulder if she were here.

"I see it's not just the guys in here." I raise my brow at the girl, then look back at Noah. He squeezes his eyes and detaches his arms from the girl, nudging her away. She gives me a once-over before swaying her way back.

Noah flashes a tight-lipped smile gesturing me to come inside, his expression dying as my eyes roam around the living area. It's too dim and smoky to figure out the faces, but I'm sure I won't miss the one I'm looking for now. I can feel the bass vibrating in my ears. It makes my palms sweaty. I feel stupid being in a simple cotton dress with sweaty dust-tangled hair and takeout, which doesn't go with the population inside this room.

"Uh...Noah. Where's Adri?" I ask Noah as he leads me to the kitchen. We pass a bunch of guys on our way. Some of them look familiar and regard me with a nod before we finally arrive at the counter. I find a group of girls, and the fact that I've only ever seen them with Charlotte makes my stomach flip.

"He must be somewhere around here. Why don't you keep the takeout in the fridge, and I'll check on him, okay? Please don't drink the punch. It's probably spiked." He pulls a coke from the fridge, places it on the counter, and strides out.

I look down at Adrian's jacket, the Italian takeout, and coke, then glance over at Charlotte's friends, and that's enough push for me to follow Noah's retreating figure.

Mixing the unfamiliarity of the place with the dim light and chaos of the party crowd, it takes me an extra second to scan the living area for two sets of familiar green eyes. But when I finally find them, they burn my heart into ashes because right in the middle of the living area, I find my Adri sitting on the couch, covered in dense smoke, and he is not alone. The girl with shiny blonde hair, a pretty face, and an even more pretty black dress is straddling him. As I stand across them, with my breath stuck in my throat and my fingers clenched, Charlotte brings a joint to his lips, leaning her ample chest closer to him. Not a second after he blows out the smoke, she replaces it with her lips, and they're kissing for all it's worth.

I crash and burn and gasp a little breathless with every stroke of Charlotte's red fingers on Adri's soft brown hair, cheeks, and tight jaw. The takeout bag slips from my hand and lands with a thud. His jacket follows next, then comes the most biblical part, where Adrian breaks away from the kiss. His emerald green eyes, full of desperation, guilt, and defeat, lock with mine. I'm sure mine are glassy, and Charlotte's reflect victory and challenge.

"V!" Adrian's voice is deep. It sounds desperate as he pushes Charlotte away and rushes toward me. But I can't take my eyes away from her smug face. I trip backward, away from him, and then I'm moving, running out of his apartment and down the staircase. I can hear his heavy footfalls as he calls out my name and strings of curses.

As I reach the last stairs, I brush away strands of hair sticking to my wet cheeks. I rush through the empty hallway, righting my shaking body when Adrian's hand latches around my wrist, and he pulls me against his chest. "You can't just fucking look at me like that and then run away from me, V."

"I think I saw enough, Adri. Why don't you go back and finish kissing her properly?" I snort, wrestling in his hold. "Or you can't do that unless you dope out of your mind?"

"Hell, you're right about that one." He scoffs, poking the inside of his cheek. "But that's no reason for you to look at me like you did back there."

"What way?" I seethe, pulling myself out of his hold. I continue down the hallway, and then I am against the wall. Adrian is crowding me with his woodsy scent and daunting arms. He breathes hot against my face, his nose ghosting mine, and I feel high on the tobacco and whiskey-scented breaths.

"Like I burned your heart, fucking tore it apart, and crushed it." I shudder as his voice vibrates against my cheek. "Why are you here, V?"

I hate that he is right. It shattered and burned my heart to see his lips on someone else. I hate that it was what I came to tell him, but only when I witnessed it with my naked eyes did I realize how that would feel.

"You're wrong, Adri," I grit, trying hard to pull the walls of denial high up around us. I smack the tears failing my façade and push at his chest. "I came here to tell you that you can't have feelings for me, feelings which are beyond our friendship."

He doesn't budge an inch away from me, places his hands on the wall beside my head, and I dare to look into his red glassy eyes. Hurt radiates from every cell of his body, transferring into mine. "Talk for yourself, V. Your eyes missed the memo."

He leans closer. His lips barely touch my cheek as he drinks the salty drop of my tear, tasting my ache. I wonder if it tells him I want his lips on mine for dear life. But I can't, not when they have someone else's taste in them.

I raise my shaking hand, trace his soft lips with my trembling fingers and dare to ask, "Did you kiss her back?"

He squeezes his eyes, his lips tremble under my touch, and then he nods, caving my heart. "Yes, I kissed back, V. And do you want to know how it felt?" He breathes, releasing a dry chuckle. "Nothing. I felt nothing, no simmering fire or fluttering butterflies. How fucked up that is!"

I blink through my moist lashes, brushing his warm cheek with my cold hand.

"Adri-"

"Adrian!" Charlotte sings from the top of the stairs. "Are you coming back here? I'm waiting, you know."

He curses under his breath, and a small muscle in his jaw twitches as I pull my hand away from his cheek. Anger replaces the agony and desperation on his face in a second. Neither of us regards the blonde or spares her a look.

But her mere presence is enough for me to retreat from his closeness. My mind begins reeling back scene by scene to the one where I saw them kissing, and it cracks my heart all over again.

"I should leave." I give him a weak smile, turning my gaze toward the exit. His face crumples as I step away from him and steel my spine against the wall. In a quick reflex, he holds my wrist before I can brush past him and stands so close to me that I can almost hear his heartbeat.

"It's late. Let me drop you home." He sighs, running a hand through his hair. I refrain from taking comfort in his offer even though I know what's at stake.

He's going back to her.

I inch closer to him. Our cheeks brush against each other for a fleeting second as I unscrew his fingers one by one from my wrist and whisper in his ear, "Go back to Charlotte. She must be waiting."

Before my resolve crumbles and my heart tears under his piercing, desperate eyes, I begin moving away. I turn and shoot for the exit, my feet failing me at every step. I run as fast as I can, away from him, from the feelings I fail to accept.

I came here to stop him from having these feelings and ended up having them myself.

12 | Where My Heart Belongs

The wreckage has seeped into my soul. In another life, when not torn between two timelines, love would be a beautiful letter written in cursive with red, pink, and purple glitters or scented with the fragrance of roses and tulips. It would be a soft melody of hearts and a slow waltz of floating souls. Instead, it is the searing fire of painful goodbyes, a song of anxious feelings, and an unfettered flow of emotions.

At this moment, I feel connected to all of it, not one or the other. But at some point, my heart will make a choice, and I hope it's worth all this pain. Because while I miss the sunshine of your amber irises and the symphony of your dimpled smile, I'm drawn unceremoniously to the moonlight in Adrian's emerald eyes and the storms of passion in his touches. And I'm afraid to lose either of them.

I know I can never let go.

But I have to, someday.

***

August wind brushes over my face as I lean against my apartment balcony, my fingers clasped tightly against the mug of green tea, and my eyes look up at the looming clouds. They have stolen the warm glow of the early morning sun rays, and I'm sure my spirit crawls back into the dark corner as my mom hushes through the line. I hear a door closing as she finally releases a sigh and speaks in her usual pitch.

"I'm glad you're coming home," mom says as I ease my hold on the mug. I took a sip, wincing at the bitter taste. "Your Dad's doing fine. The new prescription seems to be working more effectively."

"I'm afraid," My voice trembles, tears bubbling. "I might end up crying in front of Dad. Why am I not strong enough, mom?"

"Hey, sweetie," Mom coxes from the other end, her voice a sweet lullaby. "It's okay to cry. You love him, and he needs you, your smiles, your bossiness, and your cries too. And crying doesn't make you weak."

"Yeah," I mumble through my shaking lips and spit the tears. "I'll be there next week."

"Is Adrian coming home with you?" She asks, and I go still. When I don't respond for a long minute, she sighs. "You guys had another fight, didn't you? I hope it isn't as big as last year."

It's the third time she has mentioned Adrian within the last five days. It's been that long since either of us has made any effort to resolve our feelings. The night I left him outside his apartment, knowing he would go back to Charlotte, still burns in my memory. He sends me good morning and good night messages every day, but I don't respond to them either.

At college, it gets almost difficult to avoid him when he doesn't make an effort to engage. And with Charlotte taking my place permanently, I'm sure it's just a matter of time until my patience wears out. I haven't missed the challenge in Adrian's eyes. He's playing mind games with me by being the obnoxious prick that he is.

"I think he has a big game next Saturday. So, he might not be coming home with me."

"Oh," Mom sounds unconvinced, but I'm right about it. Even though we don't talk, we know things about each other out of habit or curiosity. I'm not sure. "I have to drop off, sweetheart. It's time for your Dad's medication. I'll talk to you tonight." She ends the call with a kiss, and I place the device over my heart, releasing a sigh.

Dad's fine.

The new prescription seems to be working more effectively.

A smile cracks upon my lips, the first one in a long time.

***

"Why do I have to wear this?" I wave my hand at my reflection in the mirror. I look alien to myself and tug at the hem of my short black strapless dress. Olivia gifted me this dress on my twenty-first birthday. It has been hanging on my dresser since then.

I wonder how I got convinced to join her tonight because going to a party is the last thing to do.

First, the last time I was in one, the heartbreak I had to bear still lingered.

Second, my mind is such a train wreck. Getting drunk and dancing with people I will never meet again seems stupid. But earlier today, Olivia claimed that I transferred my heartache to her, and the only way to heal- is to have a girls' night out. Third, I want to get rid of these new feelings clawing at my soul and have fun for a change.

"Because this is your last chance to wear it," she scoffs, coming up to the vanity and pinching the silk on my hips. It's a perfect fit, accentuating my hips and curves in all the right places. She's right about my last chance with the dress. I'm most definitely never going for it again. "You're dressed to slay the club tonight."

I slap her hand away from my hips while brushing my hair over my shoulders. Olivia throws me a flying kiss and goes on with applying mascara. She looks sensual in a red skirt and a white cami top. I wink at her in the mirror and wrap a silk scarf, covering up my exposed neck - it will go off once I have liquid courage coursing through my veins. Tonight, I won't think about Adrian's lips on someone else or his admitting that he kissed Charlotte back. Or the fact that I sent him back to her. But who am I kidding? His images flash in my head even as I try not to think about him.

"That looks atrocious, Vio." Olivia clicks her tongue and gestures at the scarf. Then she goes on to take it off me. "It doesn't even match your dress."

I snatch it back from her and roll my eyes. "It very much matches the dress."

Before I change my mind and double-plan my night, we head out of our apartment into the wild city. I hope this doesn't turn into a fucking nightmare.

We roll into my convertible, and as we breeze past the electrifying energy of the city, I wish upon the neon lights coming from the array of numerous bars and taverns on either side of the road. Olivia turns up the radio and follows along with the lyrics of some nineties rock number, and I try to fall back into my free-spirited self.

Maybe, it isn't as stupid of an idea as I thought.

***

Adjusting my vision to the dark surrounding, I step inside the club with Olivia beside me. It only takes a minute, and she's striding away into the dense fog filmed over from the DJ booth. I shake my head as she turns my way and gestures to join her on the packed dance floor. The air around me is thick with sweat and alcohol as I maneuver the sweaty, bouncing bodies toward the bar. I need a drink before I'm tempted to join the swaying strangers and settle my buzzing senses.

"What can I get you?" The bartender asks from behind the bar. I read his name as 'Drew' on his name tag as he leaned over the counter.

"Jack and Coke, please," I shout over the pounding bass and almost lose my grip on the bar top when he smiles. He has those damn dimples, which remind me of you, Augustus. He studies my sudden change of expression. Maybe, I look too vulnerable because his eyes keep exercising my face while he prepares my drink.

"Does my smile bother you?" He asks, sliding my drink to me.

I don't waste a minute gulping down the mix as the weight of his words has more burning effect than the fiery liquid.

"No, it just reminds me of someone." I slam the empty glass down on the table, wiping my mouth with the back of my hand. "Another one, please."

"Coming right up," the bartender releases a sigh and starts mixing another drink for me. "I hope-"

"Are you sure you don't want some fruity mix instead of all that Jack and Coke?" A voice pulls my attention off the bartender, and if I didn't have a shot of whiskey coursing through my veins, I would never turn my head to Alex. We had gone out exactly once, on a date in our first year, and it was an utter failure. Adrian had crashed our date night with Chloe, Alex's ex, and apparently, Alex wasn't over her yet.

"Alex Kennedy," I sing as he settles on the barstool beside me. The material of his denim jacket brushes my bare shoulder lightly, and his knees touch mine as he faces me. "You sure Chloe isn't around? She would love to have fruity mixes with you."

Drew passes my drink on time, and I give him my card to pay. Meanwhile, Alex seems to be calculating his next comeback. His gray eyes watch me intently as I bring my lips to the glass and swallow down the content inside.

"Let me buy you a drink," he says, running a hand through his blond hair. "As an apology for the last time."

My mind goes back to our first-ever date. I remember the smug smile on Adrian's face as he ruins my night, and all of a sudden, I want to take Alex's offer. "Fine, but I'm not in for a fruity drink.

Why don't we fix the air between us with a round of tequila shots? I will pay."

"Sure," he nods and looks away with a smile to place his order. "Four tequila shots, mate, and add that to my tab."

"Hey," I clip, huffing at him. "I said, I'm paying."

"It's my apology, Violet. I shouldn't have left in the middle of our dinner, and that too with my ex. God, that was such a douche move," he says, massaging his temple.

"Yeah, it was." I laugh, and that makes his smile grow. We become comfortable as the bartender hands us our shots with a salt shaker and slices of lime. We fall into a light conversation as the effect of two glasses of Jack starts creating a carefree sensation inside me. Besides, I have always admired Alex for his thick blonde curls that fall over his forehead when he talks and his flirtatious nature.

Two shots down, and we are laughing together at a guy who got punched by the girl he was trying to grope. Then we're talking about our disastrous date night and how we used to be good friends before that. We were never going to work anyway. He was just a chance to rebound for me, just like I was his, and I'm glad we didn't go on with it.

"You look good tonight." Alex gives me an appraising look while he shakes a little salt on the back of his hand and passes me the shaker. His eyes slowly travel down my neck as I remove the scarf and place it on my lap. The warmth of liquor and the sultry atmosphere had asked for that move, but I think it might not be the right move. He doesn't look long enough to make me uncomfortable, though. I shake salt on my wrist and lift my shot in a toast. His gaze is back on my eyes.

"To a much-needed apology," he says with a wink and taps his shot glass with mine. Then we lick up the salt, shoot down the tequila and suck on our lime.

"Again," I slur, sliding the shaker back at him. We hold each other's gaze for a minute as I try to think why Olivia hasn't joined me in the bar yet. I scan the dance floor for the familiar girl in a red skirt and white cami. But instead of that, I'm offered a vision of Adrian. I squint my eyes, and there he is, walking through the front door with his soccer friends and all that raw power radiating around him. Damn, I know he's built underneath that black t-shirt. Black is his color, and it complements his dark, dangerous personality very well. I go stiff while my mouth twists first in surprise, then in anger, just as the images of his lips on Charlotte flashes inside my mind.

As soon as his green eyes lock with mine, he halts in his place across the bar. On cue, I turn my attention back to Alex, who has another round of shots ready for us, "Do you want to have some fun, Alex? For the old times' sake."

He looks at me with a brow quirked up and a grin tugging his lips. "That sounds like trouble, but I'm in."

I don't wait for another second as I hold up the saltshaker and ask for his hand. I can see Adrian looking in our direction from the corner of my eyes, and my nerves kick in with pure anxiety. Alex searches my face for a second and extends his hand when he senses my mischievous intent. I flip his hand over. It felt as crazy as it sounds, and the truth is, I can only pull this up under the impact of alcohol. I can feel how he goes still with anticipation as I bring his hand closer to my mouth.

His eyes burning with the heat of my action makes me hell nervous. The images of him doing the same run through my head, and it doesn't feel right. I give him a half-smile as I hold his hand close to my mouth. I squeeze my eyes tightly and curse myself internally a million times.

I count in my head to get it over with and open my mouth to moisten his skin, but there's none to touch. Instead, I feel a hot searing sensation at the back of my neck and nothing in my hold.

"Fuck off, Alex!" I hear a familiar growl followed by the familiar smell of cologne. His body flush against my back sends a pure electric sensation down my spine. I don't have to turn around to know whose fire burns over my skin.

"What do you think you're doing, V?" He rasps against my ear, his lips ghosting over the shell. The alcohol running inside me doesn't allow me to pull away from his magnetic pull. Since the swarm of people is huddling around the bar, he leans more towards me. The action causes me to jolt out of my barstool, and I end up slamming my stomach on the bar counter. Adrian places his hand on the edge, and now, my stomach is resting on his hand.

"I was just enjoying myself until you showed up," I crane my neck just enough that he can see my annoyed face. "I need to go check on Liv."

I try to push past him, but he's still pressing me against the counter. He turns me slightly to the side, and I glance at the dance floor where Olivia is dancing with Noah. He whispers, "I think Olivia's fine without you."

"And I was doing fine without you." I grit at him, blinking several times to gain my focus. I place my hand on his chest and try to detach myself, swaying a little while he holds my shoulder before I bump into the guy beside me.

"You're failing at it. Jesus, V. How much have you had to drink, and what was the little game you were playing with Alex?" His jaw tightens at the last part.

"What about it? I was having fun with Alex before you ruined it once again. Poor Alex." I chuckle dryly at him and let my soul float with the sound of the bass. My body feels lighter, and I let myself lose, leaning against his chest while my eyes take in the swaying bodies on the dance floor. I realize only now that Alex is nowhere around.

"Yeah, it'll be a shame if we don't finish that game." He looks down at me with a sly smirk as I turn around with my back to the counter. "And since your poor Alex fled away, you've only got me."

"Why are you even here, Adri?" I slur, and my head starts falling backward. I'm suddenly aware of the amount of skin I'm flashing through my short, sleeveless dress. He holds the back of my head and straightens me, and I have to place my hand over his heart to prevent bumping our fronts. "Shouldn't you be making out with Charlotte? Instead of ruining my chances."

"So, you're still pissed about it. I thought it wouldn't matter since you so clearly pushed me back to Charlotte, remember?" He scoffs, brushing his messy hair and running his hand to the back of his neck. Damn! The way his muscles flex under my palm has me feeling lighter than the buzz of the alcohol.

"I don't even care who you make out with," I spin around, taking hold of his bicep, then reach out for my shot. "Go back to Charlotte. I can take care of myself."

Before the shot reaches my parted lips, he snatches it from my hand and regards the bartender with a look. "Bring the shots with two Bud lights to my table and pass me a glass of water, please."

"Let's get you out of this crowd first, and we'll see how much you do not care," I follow where he's pointing, but as soon as his hand comes to the small of my back, I close my eyes and savor his touch as he guides me through the crowd. His arms circle my shoulder to lead me into one of the vacant nooks. There's a couch, dim light, and more privacy than the flooded open bar.

"Are you trying to take advantage of my drunk state, Adrian Hayes?" I raise my brow at him, get out of his hold, and jump over to the empty couch.

"No, but someone will if I leave you alone like this." When he sits beside me, my nostrils take in the whiff of his earthly cologne. He scowls at me, and his emerald eyes sparkle under the neon lights.

"Drink," he brings the glass of water to my lips and spreads his arm across the back of the couch. His cold fingertips brush my exposed shoulder lightly. I shake my head, suddenly not feeling very good about losing the unguarded courage flowing through my blood. His jaw twitches, and now his hand moves to the back of my head, forcing my lips to the rim of the glass, "Drink the fucking water, V."

His commanding voice catches me by surprise, and I give in instantly. He always puts my health and safety at the top of his priorities, and tonight it sends my heart into a fluttering mess. His fingers brushing my shoulder creates an exciting sensation on my skin. I take the glass from his hand and gulp down the entire content in one go, but my throat still feels dry. He lets go of my head just as the bartender places our order on the table. He hands his credit card to pay, and as soon as the bartender leaves, he turns my way with that crooked smile. I can see the trouble dancing across his green irises.

"So, about that little game you were playing back in the bar," he takes the empty glass from my hand, places it on the table, and then takes my hand in his. "It's time to finish it. Will you let me or you're waiting for Alex?"

And my pulse quickens when his thumb brushes the veins on my wrist. As if in a daze, I nod my head once, then shake it and swallow the lump forming in my throat. My heart thrums with nervous beats. I'm dying with anticipation and excitement to feel his mouth on my skin.

"Hell, V. You can't keep looking at me like that." And just like that, he pulls away, dropping my hand on his lap. He leans closer, and a smile pulls at the corner of his mouth. His dark brows were narrow in worry. "You're too drunk for this game, and I don't think it's a good idea."

God, I don't think twice as I scoot a little closer to his side, his arm along the back of the booth behind me, and his knees graze mine as he turns his body. I lean over his broad shoulder to secure the saltshaker from the table.

Several beats of thudding music pass as I curl my fingers around his hand and tug it towards my lips. I hear a sharp intake of breath as I flip his wrist, bring my lips down to his smooth skin and run my tongue over it very slowly. I shake some salt on the moist skin and bring it to my lips. His eyes don't stray from mine as I lick across his throbbing pulse and feel it thud against my tongue. The taste of his skin feels so much different than any other taste. It's rich and potent enough to pique my wild senses. He watches me with wide, stunning eyes, and then they drop to my lips as I down a shot.

"Do you still think I'm too drunk to play the game?" I ask, biting on the lime as the tequila burns down my throat. I place my legs up, drape them over his fit thighs and lean my head on the back of the couch.

He slides his finger under my chin and makes me look into his green eyes. His touch creates a hypnotic air around us, and the music fades in the background as my heart pounds in my ears. "This changes everything, V. You look so stunning, and damn, I can't stop myself anymore?"

"Then don't." My teeth latch onto my bottom lip as he brushes my hair off my shoulder, and l shiver as his fingers feather on my skin. I'm suddenly too aware of his presence, and the buzz is already gone. He reaches for a shot, shoots it down, then downs another.

"Violet," his voice comes as a mere whisper, and then he tugs at my ankle- I'm closer to his body. His fingers thread in my hair. He leans in so that his lips hover at my ear as he breathes unevenly. "You turn ten times wilder when you're drunk, my little sinner."

His words burn through my skin, and my fingers clutch the leather couch as he shields me from the crowd, his stubbles grazing my cheeks lightly. I crane my neck to look him in the eye, and all the uncertainty leaves my system because I'm looking at the boy who can make me forget almost anything in this world.

Seconds tick as he keeps searching my face for any signs of vulnerability. He looks conflicted, but his eyes travel down the column of my exposed throat and soft swells of my breasts as I tilt my head to one side. "Are we still playing the game?"

Wrong choice of dress and too bold an offer!

"Hell, we are," he rasps, a devilish smirk playing across his lips. "I'm sure you would never ask for it if you were sober, V."

"What-"

He presses his cheeks on my shoulder before I can speak my words. His warm breath creates a trail of goosebumps over my skin as it tingles with the anticipation of his lips. Then he leaves soft butterfly kisses across my exposed flesh and turns them into open-mouth kisses in no time. He was supposed to run his tongue on my wrist. Instead, he is kissing my neck, and he's still my best friend. Bringing my trembling hand to Adrian's hair, I sift my fingers through the thick roots of his brown tufts and arch into him.

"Nothing happened with Charlotte," he says, moving a little higher up my neck, his nose grazing my cheek, and I feel his words simmer down my throat. "I asked her to leave just after you left, and all this while I kept her company because-"

Framing his cheeks with both of my palms, I make him look into my eyes as I say, "You were trying to make me jealous, you obnoxious prick."

His hand moves from the back of the couch, landing on my waist, and he pulls me over to him. I love how he feels this close to me. I love the feel of his fingers on my skin. And I love the thudding of his heart under my palms as I press them against him.

He shakes a little salt on my neck where his mouth has been just a moment before and throws the shaker behind him. His mouth doesn't immediately dip to my shoulder. Instead, he gazes with deep green eyes, darkening with the intensity between us.

My heartbeat turns uneven as I glide my hands to the back of his head and guide his mouth back on my neck. His fingers tighten around my waist as he trails his tongue in a slow sensual line from my shoulder to the crook of my neck, then his lips close in, sucking my skin for a second. With one swift motion, he brings the shot to his lips and downs the fiery liquid.

"I've thought about this so many times. I don't think you can count." His lips are close to my ear. "How you'll feel skin to skin with me." He dips a little down, his nose grazing the column of my throat, and I feel my sanity shattering under this new passion he's unleashing in me. "How you'll taste on my lips."

Each of his words feels like a new life infused within my bones, sinking through the walls around my heart, and I anticipate while he brushes his nose over the expanse of my exposed skin, taking in my scent just like I'm drowning in his touches.

And I'm no more holding back when he says, "There's no other feeling as frightening as the one I have for you. No one will ever feel like you, and no one can ever feel the way I feel for you."

Those words sear into my soul because he's right about one thing- no one can ever feel how I feel for him. So, when his lips brush my chin, I give in.

"Adri, please kiss me." My voice comes soft through my quivering lips, and I shudder as he breathes right over my mouth.

His eyes darken before lowering to my lips, and as the world swirls around us, we stay still. The music mixed with the loud thudding of my heart pounds in my ears as I wait a few more seconds before realizing he's not going to kiss me. My cheeks burn with disappointment and unforeseen rejection.

I chuckle nervously with flushed cheeks and prickling eyes, trying to move away from his body. "Sorry, I don't know why I said that. Maybe, I'm too drunk to handle. God, I feel so stupid. I-"

Adrian presses a finger against my lips, making me stop blabbering. He pulls me closer to his hard body, his hands holding my hips tightly so I can't slip away from his hold. "You have no idea how much I crave to kiss you," he says, brushing my hair back to slide his hand at the back of my neck.

"Then what's the problem?" I trace the sharp line of his jaw, and it twitches under my touch.

"I want to do it right when the two of us are in our senses, and there's no room for games." His hold tightens around my neck as he brings his trembling lips to my cheek, giving a long kiss before nudging the spot with his nose. If these small touches feel so intense, I wonder how deeper a kiss on our lips will go.

"I'm in my senses, Adri." It's not a lie. This moment makes much more sense than anything else in my life.

"V," he shifts me on his lap, fingers threading through my hair. His lips hover at my neck, releasing shallow, unsteady breaths, and he is back to kissing my neck, a little harder this time. I tip my head to the side, giving him more access, and he takes it unabashedly. After spending a good few minutes sucking, nipping, and scraping his teeth over my sensitive neck, he pulls back to watch me, rendered breathless and brewing with passion. "If I kiss you, I will never let you go. You will become mine forever, and that's non-negotiable. So, tell me, do you think the two of us can be more than friends?"

My spirit soars to the outer world, and I look at his face, wide eyes. *Can we become more than friends?* Even if I deny it a thousand times, my feelings for him are more than friends. So, what can stop us? *Maybe, a tie from the past I'm guarding.*

"You don't have to answer that. I know it will take us some time to get there, and that's why I don't want to rush into it," Adrian says, brushing my hair back and tucking it behind my ear. "Once you return from home, I will take you for a proper date, and then I will kiss the life out of you. And then we will kiss every minute of the day because once will never be enough."

I nod with a smile and lean in to place kisses along his jaw. I love how he shudders and goes rigid beneath each of my touches. When I reach the corner of his mouth, I want to taste his tequila-scented lips. I breathe warmly against his cheek and brush his lips with the pad of my thumb. "You've no idea how much I want to go on that date you promised. And I will never forgive you if you don't show up and repeat what you did during our junior prom. Okay?"

"Okay," he says, his breath fanning against my lips. "But first, let me take you out of here, or I won't be able to hold back from kissing every square inch of your body, including your tempting lips."

I throw my head back for a laugh, and that's when he pulls out my black silk scarf from his back pocket and drapes it around my neck.

"Have I told you that you look stunning in this dress, my little sinner?" He presses his forehead to mine and then places a kiss across it, a most gentle of kisses.

"You might have," I smile softly and bring my hand up to ruffle his hair.

His green eyes look into my brown ones with so much love so much love and adoration. I wonder if this is where my heart belongs from now on.

13 | I Want Us to Be Sure

Squeezing my eyes tight, pushing my face more on the familiar feel of my pillow, and pulling the blankets up to my chin, I try to make sense of the flashbacks. I'm sure it was a dream, a fantasy weaved out of my drunken mind because in no world I'd ask Adrian, my best friend, to kiss me. I wake up with a massive headache and follow the startled gasp in the doorway.

"Shit!" Olivia curses, covering her eyes with one hand while holding the doorknob with the other. "I just came in to give you your car keys. I swear, I didn't see you guys naked."

Her words jolt me out of my sleepy mode, and I realize I'm not alone in my bed. I look beside me to find Adrian sleeping on his stomach with his hand draped around my waist, sheets completely off his naked torso. His soft brown hair tickles my shoulder, which appears to be exposed too. I snap my head under the blanket, releasing a sigh to be in last night's dress.

"We're not naked, Liv," I say, lending my blanket to the still-sleeping hunk and covering his back.

"Oh," she sighs, pulling one finger at a time away from her eyes and finally looking at us. "Anyway, I liked what I saw."

I glare at her as she tosses the keys to me and winks at the sleeping boy, her lips twisting in a suggestive smile. Before I can say anything else, she bursts out of the room, closing the door behind her. I fall back on my pillow and massage my throbbing forehead.

And all the fragmented memory starts making sense. I was inside the club doing tequila shots with Alex, and Adrian, crashing my fun time, then us ending up in the empty nook, me licking salt off his wrist, him licking it off my shoulder, him kissing my neck, me asking him to kiss my lips, and then him saving it for after our first date. Date? He asked me out on a date. It was never supposed to happen, not when I'm still trying to understand my newborn feelings for him.

Now what? Do I still have a best friend? After letting our feelings out in the open, we certainly can't go back.

"Ugh...What have I done?" I mumble, squeezing my eyes and trying to yank his hand off my waist. It tightens instead. The blanket slides down my chin, and something soft presses against my neck. I'm suddenly aware of his intoxicating touches and how they burn over my skin.

"You smell so good," he whispers in my ear while nuzzling my neck.

"Adri!" I growl, pushing at his jaw as the scrape of his whiskers tickles my skin. "I probably smell like stale tequila."

"No, you smell like me." He groans, running his nose down my neck, and places a soft kiss below my ear. He peppers a trail of kisses along my collarbone. It sends shivers down my body. It's not a secret anymore- his kisses drive me crazy, and I want him to kiss me for real, in my mouth. It's still too soon to go all the way because I don't want to lose my best friend for a moment of lust.

Being drunk and losing control is easier to digest. In my full senses, I know we need to wait till we are into this for real. But the way Adrian lifts his face from my neck and caresses my face with those deep emerald eyes shows me how real this is for him. His brown hair falls rebelliously over his brow. Thick dark eyelashes brush his cheekbones, and the day-old whiskers feather my cheeks.

"Where's your shirt? Liv almost drooled over your exposed body." I play my hand over his muscled back, enjoying the feel of his spine. "You fulfilled one of her ultimate fantasies."

"Noah will kill me if I tell him this." His timbre rasps, a sleepy baritone, as he runs his thumb over my chapped lips. "If I don't have a shirt on, it's because of you. You tell me where you threw my shirt when you pounced on me last night?"

I can see mischief dancing in his eyes, and my cheeks heat with the thought of me going wild on him. But exactly how far I go has me blushing furiously. I push at his shoulder and scramble off the bed. My feet land on the soft material of his t-shirt lying beside the bed.

"So, did we?" I ask, picking up his t-shirt but sitting on the edge of the bed, unable to face him.

"Did we do what?" He whispers in my ear, removing the strands of hair from my shoulder and placing his chin. "Don't tell me you don't remember anything?"

"Stop playing with me, Adri," I twist around to face him and throw the shirt at his face. He releases a throaty chuckle, then pulls me towards his massive, exposed torso, and the next thing I know, our heads are hanging from the other side of the bed.

"I'm not playing, never with you." His calm voice has hidden depths in them as he holds me above himself, placing his hands around my waist in a most possessive embrace. "Do you at least remember what you said to me in the Uber back home?"

"I remember how you crashed my fun time with Alex," I comment dryly, pushing at his chest to get away from his gorgeously arousing body, but he doesn't budge.

"And do you remember the game we played after that?" His lips twist into a lazy smirk.

"Yes, yes, I remember doing tequila shots with you–"

"And you asked me to kiss you here," he says, running his warm thumb over my bottom lip, making me suck in a breath, and continues, "in the club, then in the Uber as you created this beautiful artwork on my neck."

My eyes bulge as I move them toward his neck and see the evidence of my violence. "Oh my god, did I...?"

"Yes, and for the missing shirt," he gestures towards the black material, and as my gaze shifts from the shirt he was wearing to his body, I feel like digging my grave. The fading scratches on his shoulders buzz my head with the flashes of my wild action the previous night before. "I'm pretty sure you asked me not to wear them around you."

"Did I do that to you?!" I point at the pink marks on his shoulders and then the slightly blotchy skin of his neck. My cheeks burn with embarrassment, and I'm sure they're a deeper shade of pink by now.

"You did," he says, placing a finger under my chin and making me look into his sea-green eyes. "And I won't mind if you did that again when we're sober."

I push his finger away from my chin and look down to run nervous circles on his chest. "So, did we...did we like-"

"Did we have sex?" He completes me without a stutter and scowls at me.

"Adrian!" I slap his bicep and grit my teeth. "You don't have to be smug about it. Just tell me if we crossed some lines."

A low laugh rumbles from his chest, and he holds my face in his hands, laughing some more. "You know, if we did, you would feel it in every cell of your body. Thankfully, I'm a gentleman, or you would've seduced me in the Uber ride itself."

"Oh, thank god!" I relax against him and smile, releasing a sigh.

"But do you not remember what you said on our way home?" He tugs my face closer to his, making me shudder as his breath fan over my heated face.

"What did I say?"

"You said," he rasps against my cheek, then brushes his nose, and I remember every single touch we shared. Then he goes on to complete, "I want you to f-"

"Adri!" I slap my palm over his mouth before he can complete it and blush profusely. "I did not say that, you obnoxious prick."

He winks at me, then throws his head back and laughs. I yelp as I feel a warm, wet sensation on my palm placed over his mouth.

"Did you just lick my palm?" I gape at him, pulling my hand away from his mouth.

"You weren't complaining last night." He grins cheekily, tapping a finger on my nose. My jaw drops open with sheer disbelief.

"You are something, Adrian Hayes. Just let go of me. I need to pack for the trip home." Before his playful eyes flutter my heart into a non-functional creature, I push off his body and climb off the bed.

"Hey, wait!" He rolls off the edge and grabs my wrist, pulling me back to himself. The vulnerability mapped on his face works like a magnet. I stand in front of him from where he sits on the edge of the bed. He pulls me closer, still keeping a firm hold on my wrist. His laid-back personality fades in a second and replaces it with a sudden edge of urgency. "Do you regret what happened between us?"

I look anywhere but his desperate eyes and try to subside the anxious feeling. "I don't regret a thing, Adri. But that's what's wrong here. Are we still friends? What if we mess this up and never come back to how we are-were?"

"Look at me, V," he says, brushing away the strands of hair draping my face and touching my chin, nudging it upward. I've no option but to look at him.

"I meant everything I said last night," he says, with a deep timbre of certainty.

"I do want to take you on a date, but I want you to be sure about this, about us. I want to kiss you, but I don't want to rush over it and spoil any chance of a deeper connection. And if we mess up this new thing between us, it doesn't have to ruin what we already have. You're my anchor, my best friend, and practically the only girl who can break my heart and still reign it."

My lips part on a stalled breath, catching a gleam of warmth in his ocean eyes. "You want me to be sure about us?"

"Yes, very much." He stands, pulling on his t-shirt swiftly, then tips his head down, studying me. My eyes capture the marks I've left on his neck and move toward his messy hair, standing out in all directions. Almost on instinct, I reach out to brush them off of his forehead and chuckle when they behave rebelliously. He holds my hand when I pull away and kisses my knuckles. I'm again into his spell, but unlike last night, I can feel a tug at the back of my mind, a shadow of uncertainty lurking inside my heart. As if he can read it on my face, he holds my shoulders and swivels me toward the dresser. "Stop thinking much and get ready. I want to get something for mom before you head home."

"She would prefer you instead," I say over my shoulder as I pick out a random dress and almost evaporate when he places a kiss on the back of my head.

"You know, we haven't yet gone on our first date, and you're already clingy."

He turns me around, capturing me against the dresser while his fingers glide toward my lips in a gentle caress rendering me breathless for the millionth time.

"If it bothers you so much, just wait until after our first date," he whispers, flashing a cheeky smile.

I might not be sure about a few things in my life, but I'm about the necessity of his presence.

14 | Home Sweet Home

It is rightly said- home isn't a place. It's a feeling. As I enter the familiar threshold of my house, I realize I have been craving that feeling. The sun has set, and I'm welcomed with one of my mother's warm hugs, followed by Daisy's air-knocking embrace. My father grins at me, and I freeze at my first glimpse of him.

Exactly how much time has passed since I last saw him? His pale skin, and the hollows that frame his eyes, don't stop him from looking any less charming in his office attire. He has lost a few pounds, and his neck looks thinner when he adjusts the tie around his collar. Daisy takes the duffel from my hand and follows mom down the hall to my room.

Dad and I stare at each other, trying to show off our strengths, and then my composure crumbles, and my legs rush toward him as his strong, less muscular hands reach for me. "There's my girl," my father whispers in his gravelly voice, his glassy eyes locking on mine, and I fumble over his shoulders as he pulls me in for a bear hug.

"I missed you, dad," I mumble against his chest, sniffling and holding him tightly with my trembling fingers. He kisses the top of my head, holding me with such fierceness that it turns my stomach, his urgency so unguarded, a man who needs his daughter. A sob dies in my throat as I realize how much it will break me if I lose him forever. The mere thought of it wracks me with so many emotions, and I feel stupid to believe any of his assurances.

I had believed when he appeared strong on the calls, cracking light-hearted jokes about living for a hundred years. And now, as we grip each other as if this could be our final hug, I feel ashamed for staying away from the town for my selfish reasons. How could anything weigh heavier than the love of this man who raised me, loves me unconditionally, and holds me as if- I'm his lifeline?

Adrian was right when he said, *"We often neglect what we have for what we want."*

In this moment of truth, when I finally accept the ways I have failed him, I know that we never abandon the ones we love, who own our hearts. No matter the situation, my father deserves my strength and presence, and I decide to be the daughter he sees in me.

I keep holding on to dad's soothing embrace until it hits me - his test results. My heart hammers with so many possibilities, good and bad. My eyes pinch as I finally ask him in a whisper, still hugging him for dear life. "Dad, did you hear from the doctor?"

He holds the back of my head and makes me look at him, a loving smile spread across his face. My dad isn't an affectionate person, but at this moment, he is. He wipes away my tears with so much adoration that I feel all of his emotions in those gentle touches. He nods, brushing my hair out of my face, and kisses my forehead.

"There's nothing to worry about, Violet. I'm okay. They ran a couple of tests, scans, and whatnot, but the good thing is I don't have cancer. It's *Intracranial calcification* in its early stage, hence the seizures and migraines." He says with assurance in his eyes. "I'm here, Violet, and we'll get through this together. I'm under the care of the best doctors."

Even though I'm relieved it's not cancer, brain calcification can be dangerous, and he needs extensive treatment. I'm crying once again with worry. He's not well, not terminally ill, but not in good health either. I hug him back, letting him know that I'm still concerned for him.

"I was so scared, dad. What would I do if you ever left us? I need you. Mom and Daisy need you too."

"I know, baby," he whispers, kissing the top of my head, and I feel two more warm frames wrapping around us. Mom and Daisy join us for the family hug, making my heart race with happiness and love for the first time in months.

***

Hours later, after our family reunion hug, we are at the dinner table. Apart from Mom, Dad, and Daisy, Adrian's mom Julian joined us for the meal. It was Mom's idea as she knew how much Julian missed him.

Adrian and I had spent an entire afternoon. We were shop-hopping in search of a worthy present for his mother, which would compensate for his absence.

"There's nothing that can compensate for your absence, Adri." I'd said.

"Yeah, but there's one thing," he grinned, tipping his head towards Sue's Chocolate Shop.

Julian loves chocolates, and the way her green eyes, the same as Adrian sparkled when I handed her the jumbo-sized box, I knew he was right. Nothing warms my heart more than the bond he shares with his mother. Not just that, he shares her surname as well instead of the father who abandoned them both.

The room soon fills with light conversation and laughter. Mom has whipped up a dinner that includes every dish that's my favorite.

We are halfway through our meal, discussing some medical complications related to Dad's condition, my classes for the final semester, and Adrian's upcoming game when Julian catches the notification on my phone. It's from Adrian, and the prick has to send me a series of hearts and kisses. She flashes me a grin but then replaces it with a blank look. "So, do you know this new girl Adrian's obsessed with? He mentioned something about taking her on a date."

I stuff my mouth with broccoli and give her a nervous smile. The grin is back on her face, which seems to transfer around the table, and as I swallow the salad, they wait for my response.

"He didn't mention anything like that to me, though." I clear my throat, gulping down a glass full of water.

"I think it's a close friend." Daisy chirps from beside me, and I don't miss the playfulness in her voice. It appears they already know who the girl is, or they're assuming it's me, but I still try to keep this from them. I will until we've gone through with the date. The last time they imagined something like that, I cried in my room, waiting for Adrian, and he never came.

Turning to Julian, I find her face beaming with a smug smile. "You'll tell us about her if he shares with you, won't you, Violette?" She raises her brow and then gazes back at my phone's screen as a few more notifications pop up. All of them are from Adrian.

I nod at her, flipping my phone and giving a flushed chuckle. I don't miss how everyone around the table suppresses their laughter. I squeeze my eyes and drink some more water to subside the heat across my cheeks. For the rest of the dinner, I ignore the topic that relates to Adrian. But I'm sure every time my phone dings with a notification, everyone has their eyes on me.

As the day finally ends and I succumb to the familiar warmth of my bed, I have the rest of the week planned. I have to take Daisy for quick shopping, solve sudoku with Dad, take naps on Mom's lap, and then meet Emma over a drink (smoothie preferably, but who knows).

I stare at the ceiling, and a small smile appears on my lips as I take in the faded glow worms. Adrian had helped me stick those across the bare white of my room.

My heart blows a trumpet of war as I try to settle for the comfort Adrian has to offer while pushing away the unfurling memories, memories of you, Augustus.

Your absence is felt ten times when I'm in *Winsbay*, the town which bathes with the memories of your dimpled smile, dear

Augustus. But it's also my home. It breathes with the existence of my family.

I turn on my phone and open the text messages Adrian has sent me over the day.

Adri: My heart won't stop whining. Do I need a therapist?

Adri: I think it wants to feel you around.

Adri: I don't think I can be without you. It's crazy. Do you think I'm going crazy?

Adri: Hell! I miss you, V.

His messages show I haven't left his mind even when I'm far. I had been in the whirlwind of waiting, an unattainable love. I'm not in that place anymore, and it's all because of Adrian. As far-fetched love feels, I'm sure I will get there soon.

Me: I miss you too, Adri.

***

"Do you remember *Smoothie Shack*?" Emma asks, looping her arm with mine as we take the familiar turn. My body stills in her hold, and my legs stop abruptly.

Of course, I remember *Smoothie Shack* and the stranger with amber eyes who used to work there. We spent many evenings sipping smoothies and creating memories. The moments are still fresh in my mind, and his smile is raw in my heart.

"I thought we were dressed up for a party, not to meet over smoothies and milkshakes." I roll my eyes, shove remorse back into my heart and force my heels onto the sidewalk.

"A lot has changed in a year, Violet," she grins at me. "Now they don't just serve smoothies and milkshakes. I think you're going to love the new establishment there."

I shake my head and laugh. "It better be a good one."

Smoothing my hands over my hair, I release a pent-up breath as soon as we are near the shack. My phone vibrates inside my jacket, and a smile bites my cheeks as I read the message.

Adri: Today's game was great, but I missed you in my jersey.

"So, you and Adrian are a thing now," Emma raises an eyebrow, taking a quick peek at my phone.

Are we a thing now? I lock my screen and give her an exasperated huff. "He's my friend, Em."

She puts her hand on top of mine and smirks knowingly. "Yeah, Adrian was your friend even when you had a crush on him."

"Can you stop embarrassing me for one second?" I say, shoving her away from my side, and she laughs.

She comes back to my side and wraps her arms around my shoulders. "In that case, we need to find you someone to date."

I bite my bottom lip and chuckle at her words. Only if she knew - I already have a date next week with Adrian, and the thought of it makes a shiver run down my spine.

"Make sure that someone doesn't meet Adri in this lifetime."

She clicks her tongue. "Now, I know why you're still single."

I burst out laughing, grabbing her hand and looping our arms again. We have a three-block walk ahead, and I'm already feeling the dread of nostalgia creeping into my heart.

15 | Familiar Encounters

Smoothie Shack still has the same brick exterior but with a valet service now.

"Get ready to be dazzled," Emma squeezes my arm as we enter the Shack. The old setup of sitting booths and the counter serving smoothies, milkshakes, and coffee is still there. We don't settle into our usual place by the side of the window, though. I haven't been here for almost three years, but the moment I see a young couple nestled in the booth where we spent so many lazy evenings, Augustus, I feel like running out of there in the next breath.

Although, before I can act on my impulse, Emma drags me down the narrow hallway toward the other end. We show our Ids to the bouncers guarding a small doorway and head downstairs to the basement. I'm sure this basement wasn't there when we were in high school.

"Are you sure we're safe in this place? It's getting a little creepy, Em," I say, falling behind Emma.

"It's as safe as heaven." She chuckles.

The staircase opens to a space with the party crowd. It's a speakeasy. We don't have to go to the other end of the town for a nightclub. It's just four blocks from our house. It certainly blows my mind. Music and laughter spread across the dimly lit room, with a crowd resembling half of the town population.

"This is crazy, Em. I'm certainly settling back in town after college." I yell, tipping my head down to her ear. She pulls me further inside, and my eyes follow the small den-like nooks built across the perimeter, although most are empty.

"I know, right," she says, gesturing for me to slide into one of the red booths as she sits across from me. " It's concert night tonight. That's why most of the town's population is here. They bring in a new band every week. You'll love it, Vio."

Concert. Band. The words echo in my head like a deadbeat, accelerating my heartbeat. Those two words always remind me of your deep voice.

I cough out a laugh to hide the ache. "Let's not starve ourselves while we wait for the concert to start."

"Any second now," she beams with excitement. Her eyes flick toward the mountain of people around the stage by the bar, a piece of instrumental music thrumming through the room, and the lights turning dim.

Since Emma doesn't want to miss the fun, we ditch the menu and order our regulars. She asks for curly fries and salad with bud light. I settle for wedges with gin and tonic.

"I'm happy that your dad doesn't have cancer." She says, shoving a mouthful of fries and chasing it down with the beer.

I give her a nod, finishing my drink to tone down the dread that still lingers inside my head. He doesn't have cancer, but he's still chronically sick.

She places her hand over mine and gives it a light squeeze. "My Mom says he'll be fine."

Her mom is my father's neurosurgeon, the best in town. Hence Emma knew about my dad's condition even before I did.

"I'm still scared..." my voice drifts down my throat as the crowd breaks with a nerve-breaking roar, people streaming out of the nooks down to the bar, their excitement spreading across the room. The loud thumping of drums vibrates through my ears, and then the first pull of strings, the infamous, unmistakable riff of the guitar. It fries my heart, brain, and my insides.

"Violet!" Emma calls after me as I rush out of my seat toward the herds of people blocking my vision of the stage. "Are you that excited about the music? Wait. Can you wait for me, Violet!" She holds my wrist, trying to stop or join me- I'm not sure. But I'm dodging through the cheering crowd, wiggling my way to the front. My soul is gliding toward the voice I've been craving for years. The waiting has reached its crescendo now that it's about to end.

I push against the blocking bodies, shove away anyone who stops me, and finally find my footing at the front, coming face to face with my kryptonite, you, my Augustus. I freeze with my heart stuck to my throat and my heartstrings played by your voice.

"What the fuck, Violet?" Emma yells in my ear as my eyes are on the stage, glassing to the vision of you, Augustus. You've changed a lot over the years, but not so much. You stand under the spotlight, bathing everyone with your dimple smile, your fingers playing through the strings of your guitar, and your voice streaming through the mic.

Your golden hair is longer than before, tied up in a man-bun of the sexiest kind as you sing with your eyes closed. I want to look into those amber eyes, to believe that it's not a dream. You're here, Augustus, after such profound longing.

You dance again

waltzing to my broken melody

a lover who let go

but never again

if I ever get you back, baby

I will keep you this time

The fear of loss

burning me tonight

I want you back

with every beat of my heart

my soul burns for you

it burns for you this summer

A rumble of thunder erupts through the audience as they repeat after you, your melody. And like a captive to your voice, presence, and existence, I stand there with my eyes watering and my heart burning.

You ease your fingers out on the strings, placing your palm over them to calm them down as the booming drumbeat echoes against your high notes. When the final note dies out with the music, and you finally open your eyes to the crowd, and your amber eyes lock with mine, I know I'm not dreaming.

I'm under the spell of your charming aura for a few fleeting seconds before reality dawns upon me. You can't be back like that after three long years of waiting, yearning, and longing. Not when I've already taken my first step toward moving on. But one look into your blazing eyes, all my resolve breaks, and the intensity of your desperate eyes crumble any new possibilities. So, I turn away from you and run in the opposite direction when you take a hurried step toward me.

I need to run away from you, dear Augustus. It isn't our time. Or is it? I don't know that either. But I know that you can't come and go as you wish.

Pushing my way back through the ever-growing crowd around the stage, I reach our table. I can hear the faint calling of my name through the loud bass, and I'm not sure if it's you or Emma. In no world- I can be around you, is the only thing running through my mind in repeat when I bump into Emma while running out of the speakeasy.

"What on earth has gotten into you?" She yells to my face as I run my trembling fingers through my hair. "You look so pale."

"The band," I point towards the stage as mist covers my eyes. "It's him..." I take a heaving, breathless, sweeping look across the room. "Augustus, he's here."

"God! I can't believe this." Her mouth falls open. "And you're running away from him?" She asks, blinking at me with an exasperated look, and then she pulls me back inside towards the person I want to run away from, and why I don't know.

A sudden rush of panic surges through me with anticipation and outcome. My feet trip forward as I pull my hands and shake my head at her. "I can't see him, now, ever. I need to leave, Em, before I can't."

I turn, walking backward, rushing through the iron staircase, and running straight out of the Smoothie Shack. As soon as I feel distant from you again, my back meets the brick wall. I lean back on my head and blow out the breath I've been holding since I met your amber eyes. I swipe a sheen of sweat from my forehead and the moisture collecting on my eyelashes.

For three years, I've wanted to reunite with you, Augustus, but now that you're here, I'm afraid it will destroy what little comfort my heart has received.

"Hey there, Stranger."

I close my eyes, taking a deep inhale to settle the shivers. Those three words ripple through me. Turning around, I come face to face with the ghost of my past. You appear as calm as I first met you, dimples biting your cheeks and all I've missed dearly.

You're here, standing right in front of me with so much passion in your eyes and hope.

I press my back against the wall and wish it would swallow me. It doesn't. I breathe out, "Augustus?"

You step closer to me with your hands tucked into your jeans pockets. I can see a fresh set of patterns inked around your forearms. "Are you running away from me after all these years?"

Your words seep through my skin and set it ablaze. I release a low laugh, shaking my head. "Yes, dear Augustus, after all these years."

Before you can say anything else and convince me to stay, I slide past you, then race down the street and across the road, running down the sidewalk that leads to my home.

"Violet!" Your voice echoes through the isolated alleyway as you follow me, but they don't stop me. I rush through my front porch and close the door just before I face you again. This time you look desperate, scared, and so very hurt. My back hits the closed door as your fist meets it from the other side, and I'm crying ugly tears of meeting and parting again.

The living room is dark and empty, which means everyone has retired to their beds. It's good that no one sees me breaking down like this on the threshold of my haven. And then I hear your faint voice from the other side of the door.

"Violet," your voice hoarse and strained. "I can't bring back the years we've spent away from each other. But you've to know that my heart never once separated from yours. You were always one with me. I can assure you that. And if there's even half of me in your heart, please don't run away. I'm here, and I promise you I'm never letting you go again in my life now that you're here too."

I place my palm on the wooden surface of the door and try to feel your words. They reach the most delicate corner of my heart, where you stay forever. I squeeze my eyes and breath through my tears.

And when I'm ready to open the door, my phone vibrates in my pocket. I pull it out and read the message, blinking away the mist in my eyes.

Adri: I'm falling for you, V, and your smile can be my only savior.

Adri: I can't wait to be with you.

I hold the phone to my heart, and a fresh set of tears breaks through my eyes. Because now my heart is consumed in Adrian's longing, and I'm not sure how not to feel the pain of pushing you away, Augustus.

You are here, Augustus, and the way your heated gaze studied me from afar, I could feel the same intensity in them. I'm not dreaming, you're here, and I fear this isn't the right time for us either. Fate is cruel. So I've heard.

16 | Unsettled Hearts

A light tap on my shoulder bolts me out of my unplanned sleep.

"A guy is sleeping on our front porch," Daisy whispers, tightening the laces of her running shoes. She's dressed in yoga pants and a tank top.

Forcing my drowsy self upright, I squint at her and suddenly realize who would be the guy. I pick up my phone lying beside me and check the time. It shows 5:30 am, and my parents would wake up any moment. Daisy is ready for her morning run, and Dad will join the cue very soon. Before anyone else sees you, I've to send you off.

Only for now or forever?

"It looks like you both went through the same shit." Daisy pins me with a questioning look. Her gaze shifts from my face to the half-opened door separating me from you, Augustus. "Do we know him?"

"You don't, but I know him," I say, pulling myself up and darting around Daisy. I rush out of the house but turn to face my puzzled sister. "I'll handle him. Just make sure Dad doesn't know about this, okay?"

She gestures to zip up her lips and follows after me.

The first thing my eyes capture is how peaceful you look with your long eyelashes brushing your sharp cheekbones and light dimples biting your cheeks. Your back against the wall, legs spread out, and head leaning against the doorframe- explains you were there the whole night.

You wear a gentle smile even when you're sleeping. Your man bun has come undone, and your golden strands fall rebelliously over your face. I kneel beside your sleeping frame, my fingers clutching my dress tightly to avoid the urge to brush those strands off your face. Because I know behind those golden locks is a face that will always be the cause of my heartache.

"Augustus," My voice seems to have lost its soul.

You release a soft groan, shifting in your position and blinking your amber eyes open. As soon as they meet my face, I see the urgency replacing the drowsiness, and your dimples bite deeper into your cheeks. You finger-comb your hair back and push yourself upright with a loud yawn, still maintaining your heart-melting smile.

"Violet," you mumble, reaching your hand to brush my cheeks the way you used to back then. For a moment, I feel like chasing the same feeling I used to, but then the flashbacks of your heartless disapproval and the memory of you letting go- run on repeat. So I pull myself up on my feet and away from your touch, not missing the hurt in your hopeful eyes.

"You should leave, Augustus." I cross my arms across my chest and gesture toward the gate. Your eyes follow my movements, trying to seek the conflict in them. I'm sure there's none. "You shouldn't have stayed here all night."

You push yourself almost instantly and take a step closer to me. If I had any strength to stay away, that crumbles the moment your familiar scent hits my nose, and the need to hug you scratch my heart. But I hold my ground and regard you with a firm resolve. You let me go, Augustus. You didn't give us a chance to protect our love, and that hurt still lingers in every corner of my heart. I shake my head and turn around to leave. "Fine, I will leave."

"Wait," you say when I almost dodge Daisy. She watches us by the door with a confused look on her face. "Violet, I need to..." your voice, a little shaky. "I-I need to tell you that..."

I wait to hear what you need to tell me, but you stare at me with a gloomy face.

"I know I shouldn't have ghosted you all these years, but-"

"Great, if you know, then it's settled." I spin around to avoid your pleading eyes. "I don't want you to apologize. Nothing can change the fact that you disappeared on me without a goodbye and cut me out completely."

"I didn't want to." You blow out an exasperated breath, and I can feel the warm exhale on the back of my neck. You're close to me, and it only makes my heart anxious. I turn to face you, and the sadness inked on your lips further destroys me. "I'm just asking for one chance, Violet." Your lashes lower, then rise to hold my heart. "If what we had still matters to you, please let me explain."

I'm weak when it comes to you, Augustus, but I need to think for someone I've promised. I'm tempted to give you his share of chances, but Adrian's ocean blue eyes rattle in a bright corner of my heart, and I can't lose him. It will break him.

"I can't," I croak out, knowing I can and maybe I should, but trying otherwise. "It's too late for that."

You reach out to brush away the lone tear trailing down my cheek, and I let you this time. "It's never too late for true love if you're willing to chase it with all your heart."

"I'm moving on." I walk away, back into the safe shelter of my home. I shake my head vigorously as my eyes flick toward Adrian's house. "You let me go, and you can't just come back after three years thinking everything will be back like before. Are you even here to stay? What if you didn't meet me yesterday? Would you still seek that chance you're asking for?"

You release a wet-sounding exhale, your eyes turning glassy, and take a slow step toward me. "Violet, I-I'm ready to answer all your questions, but don't walk away from me. Please." You may convince the Violet, who's been waiting for three years, but the

Violet, who wants to reach the moonlight instead of your sunshine, revolts.

I take another two steps backward, bumping into Daisy, whose gaze shifts from my face to yours as it hardens. "I think you should leave before Dad wakes up. He doesn't like guys who sleep at our doorsteps without his knowledge, and he's an attorney. Just so- you know."

"That's enough, D," I clip, pinching my eyes. Against her will, I squeeze her elbow and push her inside the house. I swivel around to face you and notice when you wet your lips, restricting the urge to plead with me again.

"Please give me some time, Augustus. I..." I say, my voice cracking. "I don't want you here, now."

"Take all the time you need, Violet. I'm not going anywhere. I'll be here, waiting for you." You keep walking until you are close enough that our forehead touches, a feather-like contact but enough to turn me to mush. My eyes flutter close as your hand reaches for my hair and tuck it behind my ear.

"Once you've made up your mind, please meet me where our hearts were united for the last time before I let you go. Because I sure as hell am not letting you go this time. Not unless you ask me to."

Once upon a time, I would've begged you not to let me go, but not now. Not when that's what I want you to do. Not when you've hurt me once so deeply that I can still feel the ache.

This time you pull away from me first, shoving your hands inside your jeans pockets and walking out of my front porch backward. I don't miss the sad, desperate smile on your lips as you slowly turn around and disappear down the sidewalk.

With my heart slamming against my ribcage, I walk back inside my house and then race up the staircase to my room.

Why does love hurt so much in all its forms?

***

I never really let go of you, even when there were plenty of reasons to do so. I did everything to keep your memory intact and kept reliving our moments every now and then. It's hard to explain how difficult it is to forget the feelings for someone you once so closely knew. We were strangers when we met, but we connected in a way I never did with anyone else before you. It was new and worth saving.

Feelings aren't like letters or journals. You can't write them off and turn another page- they linger, slowly brewing in the backburner. Maybe, over time, you get used to the low hum, but you can't seem to shut it off, and at a certain point, it chases you back.

Like now, as I try drifting away from your memories, I'm further drawn toward them. I sit on my bed with the box full of our moments, the ones I spent with you and the ones I lived in longing.

My old Id card, the first sign of our connection, your brown bomber jacket with the warmth of your embrace. The pile of napkins with the numbers of different town girls who visited *Smoothie Shack* for you. You gave me those to trash them, but I kept them anyway.

The mixtape you made for me with your songs looks at me desperately. I remember listening to them for months, on repeat, until the longing became unbearable. I had to put them away in this box. And lastly, the blue and violet journals I put away only recently. I kept them on my bedside table. Then suddenly, Adrian started showing up on those pages.

I pick up the journal that belongs to you and lightly finger the spine. The blue-colored journal holds so much of us. I flip it open, and your voice echoes from all those years back. And it feels like I'm living it over again.

"You deserve so much better than me, Violet. I would be the most selfish guy if I bound you with me. In a few months, you will go to a new place, start a new life and live your dreams. While I will still be here in Winsbay, working multiple jobs, paying my father's debt, and all the other things holding me to this town." You squeezed your eyes for a second, and when you opened them, they were red.

"I don't care about anything, Augustus. All this doesn't stop you from having feelings for someone." I said, tightening my hold on your hand.

You released a deep sigh, brushing my cheek with your thumb, a gesture I loved only from you.

"I do have feelings for you, Violet. I feel so alive with you that I want to be everything you deserve. And I will, one day, I promise. But till then, I have to let you go so that you soar in the world out there without something or someone tying you down here." You said, pressing your forehead against mine.

"Don't do this, Augustus," I mumbled.

"I don't want to, but I have to do this for you. Maybe one day, when we meet in a different circumstance, not like strangers but like our true selves, we will make this work. I will fight for you then, and we will be together." You breathed, giving a deep kiss on my forehead.

"What if we never get that chance again?" I snapped at you. Your eyes remained calm as you stared at me and said nothing. I hurried out of the truck, slamming the door loudly after me, and laughed dryly. It was so savage of you to decide for me when it was my decision too. You were older than me, wiser than me, and a lot more patient, but you weren't brave enough to admit your feelings.

Is this our chance? You're ready to fight for us, but I'm not sure what I want anymore. Back then- I believed we would meet again, and I will fight for you too. But the truth is I am not that seventeen-year-old Violet anymore. Now I have promises to keep and feelings to resolve with one that I am willing to give our chance in a heartbeat.

Adrian.

My plea heard, my phone chimes pulling me away from you and dragging me out of my scalding past. It's a text from Adrian. Last night I was so consumed by your presence knocking at my door that I didn't respond to his messages, and even now, as I stare at the words on my phone's screen, I'm unable to type in a response.

Adri: I just woke up to a lovely sunrise, but it wasn't the same without your cute snores.

A wet chuckle breaks through my lips as I finally punch in a reply.

Me: Hey, I don't snore.

Adri: I knew that would earn me a reply. You made me wallow in heartache by keeping my messages on seen last night.

Me: Is this some revenge, you vindictive prick?

Adri: I'm not vindictive. I love your snores. Fucking music to my ears, V.

Me: Are you flirting with me, Adrian Hayes? ;)

Adri: Maybe. Also, I got something for you, and I think you'll love it. Waiting for this week to end soon. :(

Me: I can't wait for the surprise. :)

I lock my phone and toss it aside. I blame Adrian for a lot of my misery. If not for his denial of my feelings, I wouldn't have met you, Augustus. And maybe, my heart wouldn't split into two if it weren't for him.

Augustus, you were supposed to be my first love, my first kiss, and my only chance. Instead, you let me go, left my heart in pieces, and now you're back, but those pieces are already with someone else, *Adrian.*

The damn ache is back, and before I know what I'm doing, I pack everything back inside the box, every trophy, the painful memory, and journals. Once I close the lid, I've made up my mind, the choice.

I scramble off my bed and text Emma with trembling fingers, ignoring the constant echo inside my head.

Me: Em, can you pick me up in the evening? I might need you to drive me somewhere.

As I wait for her response, my eyes linger on the brown memory box I've preserved all these years. How can I not feel broken all over again? Can I have the heart to do what I'm about to and still be happy? Not sure if I can do it without feeling the pain in every cell of my body.

17 | The Chance

The familiar old brick facades stare back at me as we near the *Ghost Estate*. That's what they call it now. The crisp evening air fills my nose as I roll down the window to clear out the suffocation in my lungs.

"Do you want me to wait for you here?" Emma asks, sliding down the window as I step out of the car.

I look down at the brown shoebox in my hands and contemplate for a second before shaking my head. "This may take a while, Em. Don't worry. I'll be fine."

She chews on her bottom lip, eyeing the box. "Are you sure about that? Don't you think it's a bit harsh? You can always keep the memories, you know."

I nod with fake resolve, but her words form lumps in my throat, and I reconsider my decision. She's right. The contents of this box have been the only source of connection between you and me. My fingers tighten around it as I step through the wrought iron gate of the building and race up the stairs.

The musty odor of the damp siding brings back old memories, sweet and painful ones. The last time I stepped into this place, I lost you and got heartbroken. I am back here, ready to replay that moment and get my heart broken again.

Without dallying further, I trek down the corridor, counting the rooms until I reach the one I'm looking for. Inside the room, I come to a stop so fast that my breath veers out of me. The last of the setting sun illuminates the interior enough for me to look around. I take a deep relaxing breath that I don't find you here, but it hitches as my eyes circle the room.

It's no more empty. There are signs of human establishment or just one person in particular. There's a bed with a mattress sans the sheets and a small study table, and the room is relatively cleaner than I last saw.

I place the box on the bed and step further into the room, taking in the other living details. A guitar, leaning against the window ledge, and a brown suede trucker jacket lay carelessly over the mattress. My eyes settle on the notebook lying on the table. I pick up the notebook, run my fingers on the photograph used as a bookmark and pull it out. A gasp leaves my lips as soon as my eyes capture the girl in the picture.

It's my picture from three years back, sitting inside *Book Beans Café* and reading *All the Bright Places*. The notebook falls from my hand as I remember it's from the day- I first met you. You've been keeping my picture for all these years. I get suddenly consumed in the remembrance of all our moments. A silent sob dies inside my throat, and I fall back a step, the photograph clutched tightly in my hand.

A quiet voice has the picture slipping from my hand and falling on the ground.

"Are you giving away all my memories and taking away yours?"

I pick up the picture and swallow the ache that cements my heart every passing second before I turn around.

You're standing by the door, pressing your broad shoulder heavily against the doorjamb. I can see the darkness shadowing your face, intimidating to look at.

You've grown into a fine man that much, I can see, but the tired look on your face might be due to loss of sleep.

I avoid looking into your questioning eyes, rushing past you. As I step out of the room, my legs come to an abrupt halt just beside you. "It's better this way, Augustus."

And when I decide to walk by you, I feel your loaming presence on my back. Warm hand tugs mine gently, snatching the photograph from my fingers. "You're not allowed to take away my memory of you."

I feel the rhythm of your heart beating against my back. I remember being this close to you. Your breath filters through my hair, and I pull away before your shudders hit my skin. "Didn't think you would still remember me."

"I let you go for your good, Violet."

"Good?" I laugh dryly, shaking my head. "You have no right to decide what's good for me anymore. Goodbye."

And I do not waste another second walking away from you.

"Violet, stop," I hear your labored voice as I reach the end of the corridor.

"Please, don't go away from me like this. I-I need you to listen to me once, just once."

"It won't change anything, Augustus." I spin around, looking at you with desperate eyes. I fear if I stay any longer- I might become weak under your presence. It will break Adrian's heart. But someone's heart has to in the end. And the truth is my heart surely will.

"Then there's no harm in listening to me." You blow out a painful exhale, your amber eyes dimming with every passing second. "I can't live with your indifference. Please."

The way your plea rattles through my heart has me losing my resolve. I release an exasperated breath, taking slow steps back toward you. I pull on the sleeves of my white cardigan and follow you into the room. No words are shared between us for a few fleeting minutes as you settle beside me on your bed. I scoot a little away from you, trying to escape your familiar scent.

"My mom," you start with a straining voice, then pause to pinch the bridge of your nose, body tensing beside me. "She was my everything, Violet. My mother, my friend, and the sole reason I stayed in this town." You pause, wiping away the tears that I only notice now. *Was?* Your words rumble inside my head, and a sudden dread fills my lungs. "And I lost her. She's dead."

My hand flies to my mouth as I cover a gasp, and my throat turns scratchy as I watch you sniffle and exhale a wet-sounding breath. Your shoulders slump with each passing second.

"I was at a gig when she called me that night. We had to play songs back to back. Eric said it was big. One of the record producers from the states was attending the event. I shouldn't have kept my phone on silent. She called me so many times, and I didn't pick up. When I finally did, it was too late. She was-" your back heaves as you flop your head into your hands. "One of the neighbors took her to the hospital, but it was too late." A groan stumbles out of your throat as you grit out the most painful part. "She died, Violet. My mom died, and it was my fault."

I shake my head, tears pooling in my eyes as I feel the pain radiating from you. The Augustus I knew three years back was so full of life, but the one sitting beside me now is a living example of gloomy clouds. So, I reach for your trembling hands and hold them in mine.

"Her heart stopped, and they couldn't bring back her heartbeat. I-I couldn't talk to her for the last time, no goodbyes. It broke me." Your hands tighten around mine as you rest your forehead on our folded hands. "I could feel her presence in every corner of this town, Violet, and it was killing me. The feeling of being left alone was too much to bear."

"Why didn't you reach out to me, Augustus?" I mumble, not sure to whom, but you certainly heard that. I pull my hands away from your hold and place them on your wet cheeks.

"I failed you, Violet, the way I failed my mother. I did not deserve either of you." The pain in your voice has my heart caving. "So, I ran away from this town until I could run no more."

I brush away the wet trails from your face and lose myself in your pain as you place your hand over mine. "You didn't have to run away from me. I never let you go, Augustus, even after you did. I waited for you for three years."

"I was a mess after you left town. It took me months to finally realize how stupid I had been to break our hearts." You let out a sad chuckle, holding my hand near your lips, and before I can pull them away, you place a soft kiss over my knuckles. I am still in my place. "God, I was so happy that night. It was supposed to be our last event in the town, and then we were to hit the road. Before that, I was going to meet you, fall on my knees, beg for your forgiveness, and tell you how much I love you. "

Love. My hands, my body still, a fresh set of tears collect in my eyes, and I do everything not to let your confession affect me. It does.

"Augustus," I begin, but your nose brushes against mine, our breaths mingle, and I forget what I'm about to say.

"I don't want to run anymore," your voice is as calm as ever. "You're it for me, and I can't give back the years we have lost away from each other. But from here on, I will do anything to be by your side, even if it means standing at your doorsteps forever." A humorless laugh escapes your mouth as your thumbs circle my cheeks. "I'm tired of running, Violet."

I pull away slightly as the assurance in your voice shakes me up from inside. "What do you mean?"

Your eyes caress my face with sincerity. "I want to stay this time. I could never forget the togetherness we have shared, the love you made me feel, and the peace I get when you are around. You are home, comforting, and safe to dwell in for a lifetime." Your eyes lower to our connected hands, then rise with hope sparkling in them. "And if I have to fight for it, I'm ready, Violet."

I'm not sure about anything anymore, not when this person I gave my heart to a long time ago is ready to fight for his chance. But what about the one who stayed by my side all this time? The one who wants me to be sure about my feelings. "What if things get messy, and you decide to run away again?"

Your head shakes, and your amber burns with surety as you hold me captive with them. "Never again, Violet." You lower your forehead to mine, and I lose what little resistance I kept against you, chasing back the feeling that your presence buzzes in my veins.

"When I returned to the town again, I swore I won't bother you if you've moved on. But the way you looked at me in the Smoothie Shack, I knew there was still so much left between us. I realized I'm still so much in love with you." Your words put me in a daze, but back in my head, a voice buzzes, a deep dominant voice that belongs to Adrian.

I want you to be sure about us.

My resolve weakens, and I struggle to settle for one or the other. But I have to choose, and there's only one way to find out. I'm too unsure what to do next, which version of my feelings to fixate on. I remain in a trance until your words bounce across my lips.

"Tell me there's still us," your exhale is heavy as you reach for my face. Your palms cradle my face, warm and reassuring.

I wish I knew.

Your face closes around mine, giving me the time to back off if that's what I want.

Maybe, I don't.

Too stunned by the uncertainty, I don't pull away when your mouth slants over mine, and you kiss me as you kissed me three years back. And the longing, the hidden plea, and the passion have me leaning in for more. You pull me closer and take my cheeks in your hands as I get lost in the familiar feeling. I can't get rid of this feeling even after all these years. My name rolls off your lips so painfully that it fuels our moment.

But then I hear his gasp, heart-wrenching, shocked. My eyes snap open to meet those blazing green ones, a pained look shrouding his face. With my heart thudding against my rib cage, I pull away from your touch, working to catch my wind, my eyes still at the door where he stands. I can hear a shuffling behind me, then I feel you beside me, but none of that bothers me when Adrian releases a rough chuckle and stabs his fingers through his hair.

His gaze moves past me, his jaw tightening, then he stares at me for a second before turning away and stalking out of there. I don't look back or think about anything apart from the fact that I hurt Adrian. I never wanted to break him in the worst way possible. So, I rush after him as he rounds the corridor and runs down the stairs until we are out in the open.

"Adri, please. Stop."

He comes to a halt with his back to me, a few steps, and I can reach for him to soothe his pain, but I don't dare. He doesn't deserve this. I clench my trembling hands into fists, nails digging into my palms as a long minute stretches between us. He turns his head enough for me to see the tense veins on his neck. "I wanted to surprise you. I didn't think you'd surprise me instead." His voice trembles, deep and hoarse. "I knew you'd be here, but I didn't know with him. Guess I should leave since he's back now. Why didn't you tell me he's back?"

"No, Adri," I shake my head, taking a step forward.

Turning to face me, he covers the rest of the distance between us, his cologne mingling with my ragged breath as he looks deep into my eyes. "I fucking knew it. You would choose him over us. How stupid I was to think that we had a chance. There never was one. And never will be."

"Adri," I whisper, my voice hardly coming out of my crusty throat.

His glassy eyes make me forget everything. I crave to hug him tightly and ease his pain. But he's already crowding me, putting my senses on high alert as he runs his knuckles softly over my cheek. A set of wet trails run down my eyes as they rake over his face, hurt radiating from every inch of his built body.

My breath hitches as he runs his thumb lightly over my bottom lip, his emerald eyes blazing with hope. "Did you kiss him back, V?"

I squeeze my eyes shut and give him a weak nod. I did kiss you back, Augustus. Hell! I even felt it, but admitting it to Adrian, feels a million times stronger. The way he retreats grates over every living cell in my body and my heart. I wait for him to say something, anything, but he doesn't. I don't hear anything other than his harsh breathing, then after a few seconds, his shoes against the gravel.

He's leaving.

Fear courses through my veins, followed by a salty river pelting down my cheeks.

I don't know how many minutes pass as I stand there with my eyes closed and my heart wide open. Then I feel your arms around me, folding me back in your comfort, only that it doesn't feel the same. It doesn't feel like home, but I made my choice when I kissed you, and now I can't go back.

I have to let him go.

And finally, move on, with or without you, but not with him.

18 | Not An Option

The morning after, I'm still dwelling on the thoughts of Adrian. I know he's ignoring me. Why wouldn't he? I kissed you in front of him, and the pained look in his eyes confirmed how greatly it impaled his heart. We're not exclusive, but we're both privy to anonymous feelings between us.

No texts from him only add to my anxiety. I don't think he came back to his house last night. His window remained shut, lights out. I check my phone for the millionth time. I have no missed calls or messages, and as my finger hovers over his name, I suck in a deep breath and hit it before waiting impatiently. My heart hammers against my chest, and my hands dig into my hair every time it goes to his voicemail.

By the end of an hour, I finally gave in, brushing away the rebellious tears from my face and sending him a single voice note before joining my family at the breakfast table.

Please, Adri, don't ignore me like this. Let's talk. You promised -nothing can ruin what we already have. I can't lose you. I can't lose my best friend.

The way you poured your heart out last evening about your mother's death and why you left the town has me locked in a trance. Then everything that followed made me numb for anything else, let alone the smell of freshly baked cookies. I give a weak smile to my dad, who pats my head before grabbing his bag and heading out of the house.

"Hey, dad," I push out of my chair and rush after him as he reaches the car.

"Yeah," Dad throws his bag into the passenger seat and turns with lines around his eyes as I approach him, a little breathless. He calculates my face as if he can look through the war inside me. "What happened?"

"Do you still have that position open in your office for the intern?" I ask, masking off the other emotions from him. He doesn't seem convinced but doesn't ponder either.

"You know, it will always be open for you." He regards me with a smile and goes to brush the unruly hair from my face. He gauges my face for a second, disapproval inked in his eyes, but releases a sigh.

I give him a weak nod before he darts around me and moves inside his car. And just before he starts the ignition, he looks at me to say something that renders me breathless all over again.

"Hey, Violet," Dad says, sliding down the window. "Tell Adrian he can't just jump through your window at night. Last night should be the only exception. If he wants to meet my daughter at ungodly hours, he has to come in through the main door."

Adrian came to my room last night while I was sleeping but didn't wake me up.

As soon as Dad's car takes the road, I cross the street to Adrian's home. I need to see him. His mother answers the door looking equally worried when I ask her about him. "He has not come home since yesterday." She says, her forehead showing deep lines of concern. "Did something happen, Violet?"

"Nothing happened," I lie, forcing my lips upwards in a convincing smile. "Adri is probably with his friends. I'll check with 'em.

My heart sinks in dread once again as I walk back to my house.

How are we going to get through this?

How can he shut me off entirely?

And why can't I seem to do the same?

As the day ends, I send him another text filled with anxiety and something more than loss.

Me: Adri, can you please stop shutting me off?

***

I must've drifted off. The creak of the rising window bolts me out of my sleep, and I sit up, ready to scream, as Adrian lands on the floor with a thud. In the dark room, illuminated only by the moonlight seeping through the window - our eyes collide. My voice dies inside my throat as Adrian rises to his full height, blinking at me. His emerald eyes look at me with shock and reluctance, but his face suddenly morphs into a scowl.

He stands by the window, his face shadowed in the dark, and I crave to see more of him. I scramble off the bed and reach for the lamp, but he covers the distance between us and grabs my hand.

"Don't," he says, his deep voice vibrating through every nerve ending. His hand is cold around mine, and tension surrounds his aura. I move my trembling hand over him, seeking assurance that he's there, but as soon my fingers brush, he jerks his hold away from me.

"Adri, you're here," I croak out, unable to say anything else. A long, silent minute passes between us as I listen to his ragged breathing, near to me but not close enough. He smells like sweat, whiskey, and weed as he exhales before his forehead falls on my shoulder.

My hand twitches to wrap around him, so I move them slowly from where they're bunching my long baggy shirt. But as they come around him, he whispers in my ear. "No, V. Don't make this any more difficult than it already is. You can't give me just something when I need-I want everything."

"Adri," I say, curling my hands against my chest as I feel his pain transfer into me. "I didn't know Augustus was back in town. But then I saw him singing at Smoothie Shack, and all the memories were back. I didn't-"

He releases a dry chuckle against me, lifting his head off my shoulder and giving me a close look at his face. He's wearing the same white shirt from yesterday, his hair is messier than usual, and day-old stubble litters his rigid jaw. "It's good that you chose him."

"No," I gasp out. Not sure why the words grate my internal organs. "You don't know nearly as much as you think. I never stopped loving Augustus, and when he poured his heart out about how he lost his mother and the only family he had- I became weak. And I'm sorry that you had to see what you saw, but..." A silent sob escapes my throat, and I place my palm against his chest. "Don't shut me off."

He hisses away from my touch, and I spot a bandage over the area of his chest where I placed my palm. I reach for it, but he pulls his shirt in place and glares at me. "Do you regret it, V?"

His words make me freeze on my spot. We both look into each other's eyes, unblinking as he searches for his answers. It's out here in the open. If it were anyone other than you, Augustus, I would have regretted it till the end of eternity, but it was you, and even though I feel guilty for hurting Adrian, I don't regret any moment with you.

He takes a painful step closer to me and leans in, his green eyes glassy and full of unspoken emotions. In all the years I have known him, this is the first time he looks so vulnerable as he whispers in my ear, deep voice cascading through my heartstrings. "I'm sorry, V."

I frown at him, but he touches a thumb to my cheekbones and catches a tear licking it from his thumb. "I know how it feels to love someone for whom you're just a choice, an option. I've seen that kind of love between my parents. And I don't want it. I don't want to be a choice or an option in love."

"You are not just an option for me, Adri." I clasp my hands around his neck and bring his forehead against mine. "You're my best friend, and I will always need you, no matter what choice I make, what option I choose. My need for you will remain unwavering."

"This is a mess," he releases a breath. "I want you to know I'm not angry with you kissing him." He huffs out a laugh and curses under his breath. It forms ugly knots in my stomach. "I know you love him. I know you never let go of him and probably won't let him go. So, if he is the one for you- I won't make it worse for you."

"Adri?" My eyes prick and burn, and I feel a loud crack somewhere inside my heart.

"Fuck, V. Don't look at me like I'm breaking your heart." He groans painfully, gritting his teeth, and I can trace each angry vein on his neck. "I'm giving you an out, so you can be with the one your heart belongs to, who makes you happy. Because, in these three damn years, I've never seen you dancing on air happy. And I know you need the time and space to figure that out. So, I'm going to give you exactly that."

"You want me to be happy?" I ask as every word he says makes a mark in my mind, heart, and soul.

"Yes, even if..."

"Even if it means letting you go?" I finish him when he trails off.

"You have to let me go, V," he holds the back of my head and brushes against my lips. "You have to let me let you go."

I release a shivery breath against the soft brush of our lips, and butterflies go wild in my stomach, but I swallow the burn because he's right about one thing- I need to let go.

"God, it sounded like a movie dialogue," he releases my head and steps away from my touch.

"Because it is a movie dialogue." I chuckle, even though my heart crashes against my ribcage with the pain he's hiding behind those sparkling green orbs.

"Busted," he throws his head back and gives me a sad laugh.

Another minute stretches forever as I keep looking at his beautiful but sharp face, and I hold back the urge to bury my face in his chest and cry. Because that's what I want to do as he takes a step away, then another until he's climbing out of the window.

"I'm sorry, V," he says, pausing by the ledge. "I'm breaking another promise."

Tears flood and cascade down my cheeks as I wait for him to finish his apology.

"I guess we're not going on the date I promised." He says in his deep voice, barely a whisper, then he's out of my room, and I let him go.

"Adri, wait."

He doesn't.

19 | A Song to Remember

I lose myself in the soft melody of the guitar chords and your voice. Somehow, it's faint to my ears, but it's the only balm to my heart. No, I'm not suffering from heartache or even heartbreak. It's somewhere between these two, a dull humming of my heartstrings, a numb feeling surrounding my soul. I prop one knee under my chin and wipe the tangled curls from my eyes.

It's dark, and I can see gray streaks on the horizon from where we're sitting on the window ledge. It reminds me of the day, three years ago- you first introduced me to this place. In this exact place, I fell in love with you, Augustus. Is this it? Is this a sign, a full circle? Back then, I believed we were fated. If that assumption still holds, then why am I not feeling the same amount of excitement I felt then?

Maybe it's because I'm losing a part of myself to Adrian. Yes, I won't allow myself to regret any moment I spent with him. I won't lead myself to think that they were nothing. That would be cheating.

It's been two weeks. Adrian's playing soccer matches in Iowa and ignoring me just fine. Olivia has called me ten times, and every time I'm unable to give her a reason why I keep extending my stay. It's not like I can do that forever. I have to return, my finals being the reason.

The truth is - I am not sure what I'm running from exactly. The only thing that gives me relaxation is my training at dad's firm. It keeps me busy and away from all the hurricanes crashing inside my head.

Today, Adrian was supposed to take me on a date. I took a promise from him, and I made him break that promise. How can I ever recover from the guilt that I asked him to kiss me, then I kissed you, Augustus? My mind drifts back to the conversation I had with my mom at the breakfast table this morning.

"Adrian called me last night."

I sipped my coffee silently while my heart thrashed wildly inside my chest. Adrian talked to my mom but hadn't sent a single text since the night he climbed out of my window.

Mom sighed, gauzing my face for any reaction, but there were none. "He was asking about you."

My internal organs whined with excitement, and I gulped down a mouthful of hot coffee to subside that. "What did Adrian ask?"

She raised a brow at me and then cleared her throat. I'm sure, by now, everyone in both our families knows about the tension between us but is modest enough not to bring it up. "He wanted to know how you're doing."

He hasn't stopped caring for me. Adrian still thinks about me.

"Is he doing fine?" Words rushed out of my mouth before I thought of anything else to ask or listen to.

"He's drafted to a team." She said with a proud smile. I feel equally thrilled with the information she shared.

Afraid of breaking into tears in front of mom, I nodded at her and headed upstairs to my room. My steps paused at the last of the stairs when I heard the soft voice of my mom.

"Just give him some time, Violet." She said eyes fixed on me. "You know he will come along. He always does when it comes to your friendship."

He won't come along this time because I've ruined that chance for us.

But I'm so damn happy for him, like the kind he names as dancing-on-air happy with the likelihood that he isn't moping over a girl who broke his heart but rather moving on with his dream. He will be okay even without me. God, it pinches my stomach that I can't be part of his happiness, but I can live with it. He needs to move on and be happy.

Yes, I drown in sadness every time those green eyes sparkle with life. Adrian's doing fine without me- I tell myself every morning as I search my phone for any calls, voice messages, or even a text. But I have to quit doing this if I want him to move on. So, I push his images aside and let your song lure me back to the surface.

You are sitting on the other end of the ledge, wearing loose sweatpants and a band hoodie, your golden hair pulled up in a bun, some of those golden hair sweeping across your forehead. Your legs propped on the chair, eyes closed while your fingers strum against the guitar, playing a slow, sad tune that only adds to the melancholy.

You are singing *Long gone and moved on* by *The Script*, too fucking apt for the mess in my heart. It's been so long since I saw you play that it almost feels foreign. But one look at the creases on your forehead, brows knotting every time you hit the high notes, and those dimples biting your cheeks, and I get captivated. I close my eyes and let myself drown some more in your melody.

"Cause I still don't know how to act

Don't know what to say

Still wear the scars like it was yesterday

But you're long gone and moved on

'Cause you're long gone

But I still don't know where to start, still finding my way

Still talk about you like it was yesterday

But you're long gone and moved on

But you're long gone, you moved on."

Each word of the song scraps my heart, closes up my lungs, and pain in your voice surrounds us with bittersweet remembrance. The words in your deep voice hit home.

I needed the time and space to think through my heart. Even if there is no known equation to break my feelings into proportions and verify which one occupies the most of my heart, I try to do it. I'll have to settle for the one who makes me happy enough to dull that ache in my heart.

But you are here to fight for our chance. You are the one who made me feel loved first. Maybe you're the right choice, and there's only one way to settle that. I've already chosen you, and the time has come to accept that choice.

As you reach the end of the song and finish with a final note- I replay the painful lyrics while thinking about Adrian, his scowling face, and ocean eyes. A long silent minute passes until I feel your fingers brush my hair softly. The distance between us is gone. You are close to me, but I don't open my eyes.

"Are we ever going to talk about it?" You ask softly, still caressing my hair. *Am I ever going to talk about it?*

I consider telling you about every moment I lived with Adrian, but then an unknown possessiveness consumes me. Those moments are my memories with Adrian. It belongs only to us. Also, I've already broken one heart. I can't risk hurting you as well.

"There's nothing to talk about," I say, lifting my eyelashes enough to see the frown on your face.

"I don't want you to hide your feelings from me. You need to tell me everything that's going on in your little head." I can feel your hand tense against my hair, then pull away, just like your faint cologne drifts away. You lean on the opposite side, your amber eyes burning into my soul.

My chest caves as I release a shuddering breath. "Augustus, I'm not hiding any feelings from you. It's out in the open."

"Come here," you open your arms wide, inviting me to the safety of your embrace, and I don't waste another moment to seek the warmth my heart is craving. I shift towards you, leaning my back against your chest, and you hold me as if I'm fragile enough to break into pieces any moment now.

"The song you were playing," I mumble, playing with the cuff of my shirt.

"What about it?"

"It's sad." I twist around to look up at your calm face. "Can you play something else?"

"Does it remind you of him, Violet?" Your voice has an undertone of vulnerability as silence engulfs us in a tight knot.

I know what you want to know. Am I still here? Or am I somewhere else? Honestly, I've no idea. But the song does remind me of Adrian. So I give a gentle nod. "Yes, it does."

Your amber eyes gaze deep into mine as if to validate my words. You say nothing. The calm beat of your heart against my back is the only thing I want to concentrate on at this moment.

I've lived this exact moment a million times in my dream over the last three years, and now that you are here, I need to hold it before it's gone. So, I pick the guitar from where it's leaning beside me and place it on my lap, then turn around to look at you. "Augustus, can you play a song I can remember forever?"

"A song to remember?" Your dimples bite into your cheeks as you take the guitar from my hold and position it in front of us, your inked arms bracketing me from both sides.

"Yes, a song to remember forever." I smile, reaching up to poke your dimples, and let myself live in the moment, pausing to dot for the one I need to let go of.

You focus all your attention on me, your softening eyes caressing my face for the longest minute, making my heart beat faster.

Your fingers tuck an unruly lock of hair behind my ear. Then you are playing the guitar strings, coaxing a soft melody, strumming the tune I recognize from the mixtape you gave me three years back.

You sing, eyes locked with mine, and I realize you are singing this one for us, Augustus.

"There comes a time

A time in everyone's life

Where nothing seems to go your way

Where nothing seems to turn out right

There may come a time

You just can't seem to find your place

And for every door, you open

Seems like you get two slammed in your face

That's when you need someone

Someone that you, you can call

When all your faith is gone

And it feels like you can't go on

Let it be me

Let it be me

If it's a friend that you need

Let it be me

Let it be me."

I'm in tears by the time your song ends, crying ugly, painful tears of love and longing. Love pours from every pull of the strings. It's the most heart-melting, warm, and beautiful kind. The kind I should be falling for and coming back to every single time.

You tilt down your chin to show me the same passion in your eyes, calm yet thunderous. And when you cup my jaw tenderly, searching my eyes for the same love, I don't pull back.

"I love you, Violet. Back then, I was so weak to accept this feeling I had for you since the moment I saw you. I want you. I want us together. Take as much time as you need. But if it's not what you want- I will not force you through this heartbreaking longing. But I so desperately hope that you stay with me. And I promise in my life that I will never let you go again." You lower your forehead to mine and trail my cheekbone with your thumb. "If I'm the one you chose, then let me be the one who can help you through this choice."

My face falls because everything you say makes sense. If I'm choosing you, I need to stop punishing myself, dotting over Adrian. I lean towards you with a determined heart and hope it will fix the whining inside me.

"Okay," I whisper before your lips touch the corner of mine. You wait for me to lean away from your touch, but I don't. And just before you kiss me, we look deep into each other's eyes. I see us- you and me together in yours, but I wonder what you see in mine. Because the moment your lips dip down and capture mine, I burn with the intensity in them. You kiss me with aching passion, pleading, begging, and asking me to stay.

All I have to do is accept my choice.

20 | The Acceptance

As another week passes, I spend most of my evenings with you, watching you play hopeful melodies and sad songs. I spend the rest of the night twisting and turning in my bed, waiting for Adrian to jump through my window. Even keeping it shut all day long doesn't stop me from hoping.

I've spent three weeks with the time and space Adrian had mentioned when he let me go. By this time, I'm supposed to find my answers and accept my decision, my one right choice. But nothing stopped me from the silent introspection my mind had been doing all this time.

I hide behind the kitchen wall and listen whenever mom talks to Adrian. He hasn't stopped asking about me. He is concerned about my finals and wants me to return, not for him but for the classes. I haven't stopped either, I keep checking his social handles, and all it does is - cave my heart some more.

There are no substantial new posts except one from his last match with his new team and one with a blonde named Chloe Drake. I ignore the other two guys in the picture as all my eyes can focus on is the way she has her petite body draped over his side. My pulse keeps hammering, a bitter venom course through my veins with the thought that he found my replacement in a mere three weeks. But then, after crying internally for the entire night, I swallow the vile, nasty feeling for the sake of his happiness.

It needs to stop. I won't allow myself to be hung up on one guy while moving on with the other. It's so damn wrong, and I feel like the worst kind of person to put all three of us through my indecisive behavior.

So, I try harder, with more resolve, for you, Augustus. I let myself float in the soft melody of your voice, the gentle embrace of your arms when you hold me, and the passionate kisses of your lips. I don't listen to the silent plea at the back of my mind, whispering some hidden secrets of my heart. Instead, I let you kiss me breathlessly, trying to ignore the tightness in my lungs. I ask you to hold me against your warmth, trying to relax the cold seeping into my heart. I shut off every voice, every sign, and every memory.

But tonight is the night I finally work on my choice. I send one single message to you as my fingers drift over the dusty box in my hands.

Me: I'm ready, Augustus.

I place the phone on the nightstand and get pulled back in time. The box is from years back, before I met you, Augustus. This one I hid under my bed for the last five years. I had dumped all the letters written in bad grammar by a sappy and over-sensitive teenager who crushed on the boy next door. I trace the purple heart carved on the lid in between the letters A and V. I should've gotten rid of these memories long back instead of adding new ones to it, memories that pulse along with my heartbeat.

It's time to cut some ties loose and bind the ones that will last forever. I sit for ten silent minutes with my legs folded and my chin propped on my knees. The pain has not receded yet, and it's never going to, either. Over time it will grow tendrils and coil around my soul, but maybe your love will heal me, Augustus.

It has to.

When I'm sure it's fading, a new rush of desperation has me stumbling out of bed towards the dresser. I claw at my clothes until I find what I'm searching for. I bunch Adrian's soccer jersey with his name and a faint smell. I packed it with my clothes on my way home. The thought that it's the last time I'm subjecting myself to this torment, I discard my t-shirt and pull his jersey over my head, down my body. His smell engulfs me. And for the first time in three weeks, a warm fuzzy feeling floods over me.

"One last time," I mumble with trembling lips as I snatch my laptop from the table and settle on the floor. For the next few hours, I watch all the games I've missed, and when I catch glimpses of Adrian, I let go. I'm a mess fresh out of an asylum, tears flowing down my eyes and my body shaking with the impact of my sobs.

It goes till my eyes are sore, and I can't keep them open. I sleep with Adrian's smell engulfing me and wish the night never ends.

But it does.

***

The speakeasy isn't packed tonight, just the usual town crowd filling the bar and grooving at the dancefloor. Your band wrapped their last performance in town last night, and I wonder if you feel the same ache as me in your heart to let go of the band for us.

You are by the stage perched on a barstool, strumming your guitar and playing a number that has become the crowd's favorite over the last few weeks. You always start the evening with the same song and your oh-so-alluring dimpled smile.

I slide up to the bar, giving Terry a nod. He has grown well over the years, with his close-cut dark hair and sharp cheekbones. No doubt he owns the entire speakeasy with that powerful aura of owning the place.

Your eyes follow my arrival, and you smile, hitting a wrong note. A low laugh escapes my mouth with how you cover that up with a shake of your head. Your golden hair is not tied up, and they fall just above your shoulder, giving you a more mature look. I still can't believe you'll be all mine because the mere thought of it makes me feel guilty and uncomfortable. Those hopeful eyes pin me while you sing to the crowd, adding to my misery.

I'm going official with you tonight, but it still doesn't make me dancing-on-air happy. You frown at me from across the bar as I down the jack and coke. I smile at you and shake my head when you assess me.

You can't ruin it, Violet.

And then you clear your throat into the mic, readjusting the tuning and strum softly. Once you have everyone's attention, you lock your eyes with mine.

"So, I've got this new song that I prepared for tonight," you say. "It's a cover of my favorite number for the girl of my life. Do you want to hear it?"

A series of whistles and claps ripple through the crowd, and I'm the first to mouth a "yes" as you smile at me. "Brace yourself then because this one might make you cry." The crowd cheers and encourages, but as sadness flows through your gaze, I suddenly feel a deep ache in my heart.

You start the melody, an intense shift from light to heavy tune. And then you sing with your eyes locked on me, and I know that every word in that deep, reverent voice is for me. I find myself taking a long sip of water to prevent my mouth from drying out as your ballad begins.

"It's been like a lifetime
waiting for you.
I've been running,
Falling,
Looking for your face in every hello,
Longing for you in every goodbye.

I let you go once
A long, long time ago,
And I failed you then.
But I won't fail you now
Won't let you down,
Won't let you break.
I won't let you break.
Now that fate has conspired to bring us together,
I will do right by you this time.
Because baby, you have my whole heart
But your heart is somewhere else.
Now that fate has conspired to bring us together
I will take your pain with me,
So, you can find the cure for your aching heart,
So, you can stop running from your home.
And baby, it's not easy for me
to see the pain in your eyes,
to feel you shatter in my arms.
Now that fate has conspired to bring us together,
let's fix all that we have wronged
Because I can't let you fall
I can't let you fall, not this time."

When you finish singing, my eyes are closed, my tears wet my cheeks, and my heart breaks into a thousand pieces. Because every word you sang served as the naked truth of us falling apart. You felt it even as I concealed it from you. Nothing reaches my ear, not the cheering of the crowd. Not the music that surrounds the room. Nothing until your faint whisper pulls me through. "Dance with me, Violet."

I open my eyes, looking at your calm amber eyes through my wet eyelashes. You hold out your hand, and I instantly grip your strong fingers. I feel your warm embrace coming around me, and I shatter some more. Your gaze sweeps across my face, fingers brushing away a strand from my face, and then you hold me and move us to the beat, placing your chin on my head.

We slide through sad, unpracticed steps, waltzing in a perfect rhythm for a few minutes, and fall back into silent soul-searching eye contact. It's painfully beautiful how I ever got these moments to live them together with you.

You pull me tighter against you and continue to cradle us with music playing in the background. Curling up against your chest, I place my head on your shoulder and stare at you. "You played that song for me?"

"Every single word, Violet."

My fingers tighten around yours as you hold our entwined hands over your heart. "It's time to let go and move on."

I jerk my hand from your hold, my body tensing against you. "Are you letting me go again, Augustus?"

"No," your voice cracks. "I let you go a long time ago, and I lost you the moment I did that." You hold my face and wipe away the salty trails there.

I ball my hands over my heart and shake my head. "I chose you, Augustus. I'm ready to fight for us."

"You're fighting so hard for us, Violet." Your voice is a whisper. "But you are on the battlefield without your armor. No matter how much I try to shield you, you will still break into pieces, bruised and wounded, scarred for a lifetime. And I can't do that to you."

"Why are you saying this?" My lips tremble as I trace the line of your jaw, trying to make sense of your words.

"You need him, Violet." I can read the declaration on your face. "He's the one who doesn't need to be physically present to claim his existence in your heart."

I wish for you to be wrong about this, but everything you say seems like an epiphany. "You said you would fight for me. You promised to help me through my choice."

"You can't always choose who to fall for or who to love. Love is not a choice sometimes, it just happens, and we can't help it." You drape your arms around me and stroke my hair as my breathing turns choppy.

"I love you, Augustus." I curl my fingers around your frame, trying to hold you for as long as I can, but I know that sometimes love isn't enough to be with someone.

"I love you too, Violet." You place your forehead against mine as I whimper. "But we both know that you are in love with him."

I finally break into your arms, taking in a mouthful of air to settle the spasms in my lungs. Our hands reach for each other with equal desperation. You hold me close to your heart as we cry painful tears knowing that we need to go through this together till the end.

Because no matter how hard we fight, we can't bring back the years we have lost. We can't fill the gaps between us. We met as strangers, and we're back to being strangers, walking on opposite sides of the road. But I don't regret meeting you, Augustus. Even though it's a cruel truth, I accept that you led me to Adrian.

After we embrace each other, reliving all the moments up to this heartbreaking one, I pull back enough to capture the features of your face one last time. The warm tint of your amber eyes, golden hair that resembles the sunlight, and those dimples biting your cheeks will always be mine, even though you are no longer mine.

"You can let go now, Violet." You mumble the words over my lips before touching your mouth to mine in a soul-shattering kiss. I close my eyes and kiss you with a promise that you will always be in my memories and that every fragment of you will be a beautiful part of my story. This kiss is a remembrance. We've connected like this before, with a hopeless, breathless dance of passion. Only this time, we are finally saying our goodbyes.

When we pull away from each other, there's no remorse in your eyes, none in mine. We are doing it right this time. As we walk out of the *Smoothie Shack*, the place where it all started, I look at my familiar stranger walking beside me and smile. We were like the fairytale in this real world, but my story is waiting for me somewhere else.

Late at night, as I sleep in my bed, I recall all the moments we've created in these three weeks. They are worth all the painful years I longed for you, Augustus. And I don't know if Adrian has already moved on or it's simply too late for us, but I'm ready to fight for my love. His green eyes spark a new hope in my heart just before I fall asleep.

***

I find my way back to the old housing estate in the morning to see the last glimpse of you before I move on to a new love. The empty walls stare back at me when I step into the room where your song still echoes.

But you are not here anymore, Augustus.

21 | No More Running - Part 1

On my way back to Iowa, I'd decided to take it slow. I planned on giving myself some time or letting my heart at ease before meeting the person who makes it go wild. I failed. The moment I get to my room, all the memories, the gentle hugs, and the braiding of hair late at night while watching movies just crash into my head.

I dump the duffle in my room. And before I can speak myself out of it, I'm pulling my car out of the garage. A thousand unsaid emotions run through my head, laced with apologies and confessions due. I close the car and walk to the stairs leading to his apartment with my nerves on high alert, my heart thudding, and my pulse racing. But all of that evaporates as I pound at his door half a dozen times to no avail until security comes up and tells me Adrian no longer lives there.

After making a fool of myself, I head back to my car and realize Adrian's Harley is missing in the garage. I didn't notice that in my rush to reunite with him. Cursing myself out, I speed back to my place and make a note to get his new address from Noah or Chloe Drake if I have to.

My blood boils when I open Adrian's profile and look at her blond hair brushing his shoulder. I push the image aside and pull out the phone from my pocket once I'm inside my apartment.

Me: I'm back here. I need to talk to you.

Me: I didn't know you changed apartments. Send me your new address, or I will take it from Noah if not Chloe Drake.

In all the years we spent together as friends or more, he never once ignored my calls or messages. But in the last three weeks, he has surpassed his self-control for shutting me off. I'm sure he's reading my texts, and the fact that he hasn't blocked my number tells me I still have hope.

I'm sure he's still hurting. I've seen that on his face through all his posts and games I watched two nights back. He doesn't know I'm past my choices and back to him, and maybe even after knowing Adrian might take a while to accept it. Then there's this deep, unsettling fear about his connection to the blond-haired girl with a straight nose.

***

Olivia finally comes home to find me curled up on the couch, the tissues lying on the floor, giving her all the answers. I've told her everything about you, Augustus. That's why she doesn't ask anything and wraps her arms around me until I finally feel that pain is no more surrounding me.

"Won't you ask me how it went?" I ask her when she doesn't speak for the longest time.

"I'll not force you through the painful memories again. So, yeah, I'm cool not knowing." She says as I turn around to face her. She has a soft, gentle smile etched on her lips.

"I think I have deep-rooted feelings for Adrian, feelings that may get hurt if he chooses Chloe Drake over me." I look up at the white ceiling as another cry blocks my throat.

Olivia remains quiet for a few minutes before I turn to face her again. "You chose Augustus over Adrian, and here you are, running back to Adrian. And he hasn't stopped running away from you since you let him go and still seems to be right where he was. Does that answer your doubts?"

Her words make my heart jump with possibility, and a smile breaks through my lips after days of longing and despair. I chew on my bottom lip, clearing my throat. "Adrian has shut me off."

"Can you blame him?" She releases a sigh. "He has shut everyone out, Vio, including Noah. Most days, Adrian is busy training or partying with his new team. I haven't seen him on campus ever since he returned from home. He's a mess just like you."

My heart sinks as I picture those sad green eyes looking deep into my soul, begging me to stop him from leaving as he stepped out of my window that night. I close my eyes and sniffle silently. "Do you think we can work this one out, Liv?"

She hummed. "I think you will."

***

I search through the crowd for a tall, built silhouette with tousled brown hair and piercing green eyes. It's been another week of being shut off. Although I have Adrian's new address by now, I'm taking time to reconnect. In these seven days, I've seen him exactly twice.

Once, when he came to *Brew Story* but stayed outside. I saw his broad shoulder leaning against the door before he headed back. I handed the half-filled iced latte to the guy across the counter and sprinted towards the door. By the time I was out in the street, he was gone.

He might have seen me behind the counter.

Then I'm sure I saw Adrian's Harley revving off the curb outside my building. Maybe, it was my imagination because why would he come to my apartment if he didn't want to see me anymore?

I wait for him at the far end of the fluorescent-lit hallway that leads to the dressing rooms, and I'm already shaking violently. I ignore the sweaty athletes buzzing around me as my eyes remain locked in the locker rooms.

I've been making myself strong enough for the confrontation, and now that the time has come, I don't feel very confident. Adrian knows I'm back and still decided to remain distant. There can be only one reason for such ignorance.

Maybe, he moved on.

I'm anxious and sweaty, and my nerves are all over the place. But I'm not giving up. I'm here for Adrian, and if there's even a one percent chance that he still feels for me, I'm taking that. I ball my fists on the soft fabric of my mid-thigh cotton dress and keep taking glances whenever someone steps out of the dressing room.

Then he emerges from the locker room in all his arrogant, gorgeous, and masculine beauty. His built frame is wrapped in a black tailored suit, and brown hair falls just enough on his forehead to give him that arresting look.

But I want to look into his eyes, reach the depth of his soul and search my pieces- if they still exist. I need to know if he still makes me feel loved the way those green eyes sparkle when they find me. I try to take a better glance through the crowded concourse, craning my neck as better as I can to gauze his expression. Is he missing me in the spectators? Did he see me cheering for him? He's too far to feel my presence.

I dodge my way through the people littered in the narrow hallway, picking up my pace as I see him turn towards the exit. My breath turns choppy as the distance between us slackens, growing more anxious as I finally stumble to a stop near his group.

His new team members surround him. I have seen these guys in his recent posts. Then my eyes capture the blond-haired beauty beside him. She is as perfect as a model out of a fashion magazine, petite enough to grab attention, dressed in a classy gray dress, smiling, and talking to the group, but her eyes are on my Adrian. My heart burns from the inside out.

When I take another step closer, I realize he is not looking at her but at his phone. I sent him a couple of texts and voice messages on my way here. Is he reading my messages? Maybe that gives me the courage I need as I reach straight for him and stand in his line of sight. My cheeks are burning, my palms are sweating, and if he doesn't stop looking at me with so much intensity in his ocean-green eyes, I may evaporate soon. He keeps looking at my face without blinking for three solid seconds, and I can feel every other eye around us staring.

He's very still, his broad shoulders locked, and I can feel the chill of his cold demeanor over my skin. He's hiding his emotions, but my emotions are spilling through my pleading eyes as I wet my lips and force the words out. "You're avoiding me, Adri."

He's silent and doesn't react or speak, but I can see the subtle twitch on his lips. He looks at my mouth as I nibble on my bottom lip, too nervous for his answer.

I turn toward his group, letting my gaze pause at Chloe Drake for a second. "Too busy with your new friends, I see."

Something shifts as his eyes move from my face to his team members. "Wait for me in the parking lot."

Then he looks back at me, too many questions running behind his detached expression.

"When are you running back to your goldilocks?" He scoffs, running his index finger through the inside of his collar as soon we are alone in the far corner of the hallway.

"I'm not running back to anyone." My heart caves as he regards me with a cold, unwelcoming look. He still thinks I'm going back to you, Augustus. He doesn't know I've lost you forever.

He runs his hand through his hair and huffs out a rough sigh. "Go home, V."

He turns to leave, but I reach around to stand in front of him. "You remember when you said you wanted me to be happy?"

"You're not happy?" He frowns, breathing unevenly, and I can feel how hard he's trying not to reach out to me.

"Turns out Augustus isn't the one who makes me dancing on air happy."

His shoulders flex, and I don't miss how his fingers tighten into fists. He watches me with fake disinterest, and I know it because I've known him all my life.

"Go back to the one you chose and find your fix." His jaw tightens as he scowls at me. "He's your choice. He should be your happiness too."

"I'm past my choices, Adri. I'm not running after my choices anymore." I whisper, heart aching. "I know now that the most beautiful relationships don't always build over choices, that love is not always a choice."

A deep rumbling wave of emotion passes through his eyes as he takes a step closer to me but doesn't reach out. Then he's back to his cold self, and I see the pain in those green orbs. I can see the longing in his eyes, the same longing that makes my heart go frantic. He's not happy either, but I wonder if I'm the one who can make him happy. Or is it the blond girl waiting in the parking lot?

He bends towards me, holding my gaze until his hot breath touches my ear. "That's until you don't find Augustus strumming his guitar in some bar downtown."

His intoxicating scent renders me breathless for a few seconds, but his words cut deep wounds in my heart. He will never get over the fact that I shoved him aside for you, Augustus. And you were right. I do need him.

He steps away, giving me soul-deep eye contact, then stares at the exit.

"Are you with Chloe Drake?" I ask, following his gaze.

His jaw turns rigid as he pinches the bridge of his nose and heads toward the exit. He doesn't answer my question because he thinks it doesn't concern me.

"You said you want me to be sure about us," I stand at the exit door, hugging my waist and shaking with the impact of unshed tears.

He stops just a few inches away from me. His back heaves due to his uneven breathing. With his back to me, he tilts his head enough for me to see the hurt on his face.

I shout without caring who can hear me and making sure he does. "I'm sure about us now."

He stays rooted to his place for a long second before taking heavy steps away from me. Then he climbs into the black sedan that waits for him and leaves.

22 | No More Running - Part 2

I walk, taking a long way home after spending an hour in the dark, secluded park, admiring the view of one of the oldest suspension bridges in Iowa. I remember walking across that bridge with Adrian when we came in. We explored the city the first year when we were still freshmen. All the memories are still fresh in my mind. We've been so much together that I can't imagine my life away from him.

As I walk through the hills, it starts drizzling, and by the time I take the sidewalk that leads to my complex, it's downright pouring. I hug my trembling frame as raindrops splatter my face, and every frigid drop chills my skin and penetrates my bones.

Fucking perfect!

Then my feet come to an abrupt halt when I see the black Harley parked in front of my building and a tall, imposing figure leaning against the beast of a bike.

I stare at him through wet eyelashes, blinking against the icy drizzle, watching as he straightens. He stares up at me, our eyes catching beneath the spitting rain. And I want to either run towards him because he is here or run back from where I came in if I'm dreaming.

He looks so handsome, even dripping wet, his brown sodden strands messy, sticking across his brow. He's standing tall, with his suit jacket thrown over his right shoulder, while his white shirt clings to his muscular frame, every thread soaked. His white skin looks paler due to the rain. He moves away from the bike, stepping closer to me, and I blink at him with clattering teeth against the cold.

Standing just out of my arm's reach, he holds my gaze with a look that says it all. He's here. It's not my imagination. He takes another step, then wipes the rivers of rain from his face before pulling out his suit jacket and draping it over my shivering figure. The closeness and the smell of his cologne mixed with his scent have me take a step back. Now that I know what they can do, I can't take it without confirming what he wants. They're sure to tear down the walls around my heart and leave me gasping while he decides to move on with some blond-haired Barbie.

"Why are you here, Adri?" I ask, my teeth clattering and my voice a mere whisper.

He shoves his hands into his wet hair, huffs a haughty laugh, then holds me captive with those green eyes. "What you said about us...were you serious?" He grumbles in a deep gravelly voice. It makes me clench my hands into fists from smoothening the tightness of his jaw.

"Every bit of it," I say, nodding my head slowly, I take a confident step forward, closer, my eyes on his, and everything disappears when he finally reaches out and draws me in. He takes slow steps toward me and stops when our shoe touches. He holds my face in his large palms and brushes away the tears falling from my eyes.

"I let him go," I say, my voice shaking as I inhale sharply, his scent reaching every aching corner of my heart.

"Augustus? Why?" He frowns, his eyes running over my face, studying my features for a long minute, then he tucks a wet unruly lock of hair behind my ear. His hold is gentle around my face as he thumbs my bottom lip, and our breath quickens.

"Because I chose him, but that choice in itself wasn't enough to bind us together," I say, the warmth of his hands framing my face making it easier to confess. "The time I spent away from you made me realize that there are so many different shades of love-The shade that fades with time but remains in light tint throughout your lifetime and the shade that grows darker with time. My story with Augustus was the fairytale kind, the dreamy shade. But what I have with you is something I never planned. It just happened without any choices or options."

"What do you mean, V?" He whispers, closing his eyes for a long minute, then they pin me questioningly.

"I want you, Adri. I love you with every piece of my broken heart, every part of my existence. I think I can't be without you either. I can't be without your obnoxious self, clinging to me or your moonlight smile brightening my darkest nights."

"No, V. You were consumed in his love for three years. He is the one you chose, the love of your life." He shakes his head, taking a staggering step away from me, his chest rising and dropping with the impact of his heavy breathing. His face darkens when he looks me in the eye. "Did you say that to him when you were with him?"

My heart crumbles, dread burning my insides. "Adri, I do love Augustus. I can't deny it." I brush a wet strand of hair from my face and stare into his eyes, letting my heart out in the open. "But that love was too good to be true, a dream, a fairytale I was merely believing. During the time we spent apart, when I waited for him, I became a different person. He left me with a wounded heart, but I had already healed when he returned. I had already moved on. And maybe it took me a lot of time to realize that, but I know it now. I do."

He swallows hard, the movement making his jaw clench, and I can sense the vulnerability in his piercing green eyes.

I can't breathe. The weight of my confession and the uncertainty etched on Adrian's face are too heavy against my chest. I can't just expect him to throw everything he has done to move on just for a few words of affection from me. It's too much to ask from him. We both need time to nurse our feelings into something worthwhile- if we still have a chance to reconcile.

"It's not fucking fair, V." He releases a wet-sounding sigh, and I can see his eyes glassing. "You can't just make me feel like some third-wheeler trying to woo someone else's girl and then come back to me with your heart at your sleeve, telling me you were my girl all along."

"I'm sorry, Adri," I whisper, throat choking when I look at him. "I'm sorry for ever making you feel that way."

Adrian relaxes against his bike, his shoulders dropping as he runs his hands over his hair. The rain has settled to a light windy drizzle, and we are both standing under its harsh pattern. When he realizes I'm watching with so much remorse, he scowls. "Don't do that."

"Do what?" I take a careful step closer.

"Don't look at me like some broken boy. I don't need an apology." He says, even though he looks a lot broken. "I'm a grown adult. You don't have to patch up my wounded heart. I can handle rejection very well." When I gather my courage to look at his face, I see his red eyes and feel the hurt radiating from every inch of his body. He shakes his head with a distant memory. "I'm not that fifteen-year-old boy who saw his best friend in a yellow summer dress and realized he might be having feelings he shouldn't have towards his friend, then panicked with the thought of losing her and lost her anyway. I'm not that boy who panicked taking his best friend to the junior prom because he panicked yet again to lose his shit and sabotage the only person who knew how not to make him feel broken. I'm not that boy, V."

I blink, my breath hitching at his confession, loud. "Adri-"

I take a step closer to him. "Did you always have feelings for me?"

He strengthens and swallows hard as I take one more step.

"Why do you think no one from our high school approached you for a date?" he asks, voices a little sharp, but I don't miss the subtle smirk.

"You're an asshole, Adrian Hayes," I say, covering the rest of the distance between us and glaring at him. "Why did you let me believe I was the last girl you would choose?"

He leans down, dripping with icy water, and holds my face again in warm hands. "It scared me to lose the only girl who meant the world to me over my teenage feelings. I thought maybe it was just some hormonal disbalance. But damn, was I wrong?" He cups my jaw and runs the pad of his thumbs over my cheekbones. We are both a crying mess. "I'm not angry with you, V. I love you so much that I want to be the one who deserves you. I want to be a worthy choice, a better man for you. And I'm sorry for not turning off my feelings when I should have and putting you through this choice."

"None of this is your fault, Adri," I say, clasping my hands around his neck and bringing our foreheads together. "This one's on me. And don't ever think you're not deserving. You deserve every goddamn piece of my heart." My voice fills with the scorching rays of the summer, burning me up tenfold. "Because you were the first boy who made my heart flutter, Adrian Hayes."

A long silent minute passes between us then he drops his forehead against my shoulder, breathing harshly. "I'm leaving for Minnesota tomorrow." He says, voice cracking as he releases a sigh.

I can hear a crack inside my chest, almost like rich china. But I'm not fragile. I'm a living, breathing human. I need to heal, and so does he. "Promise me you won't shut me off when you reach there." I brush our noses together. "Promise me you won't stop yourself from finding that dancing-on-air happiness."

He pulls away. "When I said - you're the only girl who can break my heart and still reign it. I meant it, V." He tugs me to his warm, familiar body, the one that feels like home, and places a chaste kiss on my forehead. "We both need time to heal, my little sinner.

And I hope you know that you're the only girl I ever loved and love, but I certainly don't expect to be the only boy in your life."

"God," I breathe out, our breaths mingling. "Make one last promise to me." I tighten my fist over the soft fabric of his shirt. "Maybe one day, when our hearts are healed, and we've run past all our choices, we will find our way back to each other and fight for our story. And when you're ready, I'll be waiting."

"I promise, V," he smiles at me, our eyes turning glassy. "I will never let you go."

"Me neither," I croak out, smiling, and not a second later, I feel his lips back on my forehead. His arms wrap around me for a long, calming embrace before he slips away from my touch while I watch him leave with sad but promise-filled green eyes.

I'm in love with you, Adrian. And no matter whether our broken hearts heal or not, I will still choose you.

23 | A Love Song

One year later

Adrian

She is my miracle, my constellation, and my love song. Her smile saves me from drowning in chaos. The twinkles of her brown eyes brighten my darkest night. I hear her voice as the melody that always lifts my spirit.

She's my soulmate, my Violet.

Stubborn strands of her chestnut hair fall on her face, and she scrubs her nose. I want to brush them away, but I don't want to wake her up. She doesn't know I'm here. It's her twenty-fourth birthday, and this is what she wanted as her present.

"What's your wish for this birthday, V?" I had asked over the phone while running across the field. It was 5 am, and we'd been talking for five hours straight. The fact that we hadn't slept the whole night affected my muscles.

"How about you as my birthday present?" She said, and I didn't miss the playfulness in her voice. Then she cleared her throat, hiding that she unknowingly spelled what was in her heart. "I was kidding. Just Facetime me after your game."

So, here I am, in her room, lying beside her on her bed. With her only an arm's reach from me, my heart won't stop thudding, and my soul aches to gather her in my arms. It's been months since I breathed her scent and embraced her. Thick eyelashes fanning towards sharp cheekbones and kissable lips pulled together in an adorable pout- she looks so beautiful that I revel in the feeling of her beside me instead.

The moon gleams silver through the window she left open tonight. Is that a coincidence, or can she read my mind? I call it my luck. The second I arrived in the town, I wanted to run to her house and see her pretty face. But I decided to give her a surprise birthday present. She will be pissed, but I want to kiss her breathless even more when she has those streaks of fire in her eyes.

It's been a year since she's been in town, training under her dad, and I'm playing soccer around countries. Although we belong to two different worlds now, our hearts belong together. Because no matter where I go, I keep coming back to her, my Violet, my home. I move the strand of hair covering her face with my index finger and tuck it behind her ear. She squirms a little in her sleep and moves an inch closer to me.

I inhale sharply as her breath mingles with mine. My willpower turns to ashes with every whiff of her familiar scent. I am too weak when it comes to her. I cannot stay away from her another minute, another second. It's pure brutality.

Composing my uneven heartbeat, I twist my head on the pillow, admitting she is finally in front of my eyes, curled up beside me, lost in her dreamland. Her hands move over mine. She pulls my hand and tucks it under her face. She looks so content, peaceful, and happy that a sob forms inside my throat. A deep frown appears on her face, with her eyes closed but her eyebrows pulled together. Then her dark eyes blink open. The moment the fog of sleep clears, she stares at me like I'm a ghost, only that I'm not.

Violet

The feel of his warm skin and his familiar scent seem too real to be a dream. I wake up abruptly, trying to calm the race of my heart, and open my eyes into the darkness of my room to those ocean-green eyes. His uneven breaths tickle my face to my right. It's not just a dream because I feel them too.

I lay still, blinking at his handsome face, which has turned sharper over the years. He still has the same brown, messy hair, a little close-cut now, but they make him look like a grown man. He tugs his lips upward into a beautiful smile, and I start sniffling. I place my palm over his warm cheek to confirm I'm not dreaming.

"You're here, Adri," I whisper, my lips trembling under the impact of my ragged breathing.

"I'm here, V." He frames my face in his large hands and nudges our noses together, and within a second, I'm up and in his arms. I cling to his body, sobbing into the crook of his neck. I'm sure we may run out of air supply if I keep holding on to him like this.

"I missed you," I mumble against his ear, then I sob.

"God, I missed you so much, V," he groans, pulling me closer to his body, and I don't care if someone walks on us right now, but I keep crying against his neck like a baby.

"Why didn't you tell me you were back in town?" I pull away enough to capture the features of his face as he runs his thumbs over my wet cheeks and places a deep kiss on each of them.

"It was your surprise birthday present, silly." He laughs through his glassy eyes and pulls his lips into a playful smile. "Tell me you love it."

I slide closer to him, and he rolls us, leaning over me, balancing his weight on his elbows. I cup his face and pull him down, our foreheads touching, noses too. "I do, and I love you, Adri. Tell me you're staying." I sound desperate, needy, and weak, but I don't give two shits about those emotions. Because staying away from him, knowing I'm so deeply in love with him, was like a death sentence for me, and he's finally here to save me.

"I'm staying here with you forever," he breathes, then leans down and tilts his head to press his lips to mine. It's a feather-like touch. "I want to fulfill my promise. I want to take you on that date, and nothing can stop me from kissing you this time."

His words render me breathless all over again. My eyes fall on the dog tags clinking together as they dangle above my face, and I catch a letter V on one of them. I reach for them, and there it is, the letter V on one side and A on the other. When I search his eyes, I see how his cheeks turn a shade of pink, and he tries to snatch the dog tags from my hold. And that does it. I hold the back of his head and bring his mouth to mine.

But before our mouths can mold together, he speaks against my lips, a little breathless. "Are you sure, V? We can wait till our date. I want this moment to be perfect."

"This is perfect," I mumble, already losing myself in the moment. "I don't want to wait. No more waiting, please."

"If I kiss you, I won't let you go ever," he runs his thumb over my bottom lip and places a slow, open-mouth kiss on the corner of my mouth. "I will lock you up with me and keep you to myself."

I release a low laugh, holding his gaze. "Oh yeah, and what are you going to do then?"

His green eyes turn a shade darker, a devilish glint running in them. "Whatever I want and whenever I want."

"I need..." My mouth turns dry under the intensity of his gaze. "I want you to kiss me." And he doesn't waste another second to hold the back of my head as he devours my gasp. The kiss is as powerful as his grip on the back of my neck. It makes me breathless, the intensity of the naked truth in this new feeling, in kissing someone you know has been waiting so long to kiss you and who wants to kiss you. There's nothing gentle about how we're learning, exploring, and living the kiss. It's everything, fireworks, explosions. Then his kiss turns tender as he licks across my lips, parts them with his tongue, and explores every corner inside my mouth. I do the same. He tastes like life, death, afterlife, and rebirth, a full circle. His hand moves to brush my cheeks, hold my nape, and pull me more against him.

When he stops kissing me, we are both breathing heavily. He holds my eyes for seconds before the first tear falls on my cheek. I tug his face down, and we kiss again, only this time we taste the salty confessions, the pure agony of separation through the kiss. I lift my hands to tangle my fingers in his hair, soft as I remember touching them so many times before, then curl my hand around his nape and let myself dissolve in the warm, fuzzy feeling of arousal taking over us. Adri never does half-assed things. And this is evident through how he shifts above me, bracketing me between his tensed biceps while I feel his desire hot and hard against my hip.

We break from the kiss, and he shifts away, pulling his hips back. The veins lining his neck tell the story of his restraints finally coming loose. At least I don't hold back my emotions for him anymore.

"Fuck, that was hot," I mumble across his lips, panting. "Where did you learn to kiss like that?"

"Do you want me to teach you?" He groans, nibbling on my bottom lip while his fingers trail across my belly and touch the exposed skin lightly. I shiver underneath him, his touch working as raw fire all over my body.

"Sure," I breathe, tugging his t-shirt up, and he pushes away a little to help me pull it off him. My eyes instantly capture the pattern over his left breastbone, and I know what it resembles in a flash. He follows my gaze, and I use the moment to flip us over.

I run my fingers over the little flower inked over his skin, my eyes turning glassy. It's a Violet.

"Is that a Violet?" I ask, looking at him in awe. "When did you get this?"

He reaches up to frame my face in his warm palms and pulls me closer to his body. "It doesn't matter when I ink it over my skin. My Violet has been inside my heart for a long time now."

Then his lips are back on mine, and this time, we take slow, languid sweeps across each other's mouths. And at this moment, I remember the day he walked through my window, and I broke his heart. That day he had a bandage over his chest.

But I don't let myself regret any of the moments I lived with you, dear Augustus. Instead, I thank you for being the reason I'm finally with Adrian, my anchor, my rock.

He smiles. It's bright and fiercely stirs my insides.

"When I think about it, I never had a choice." I finally admit.

He pauses at my confession, and his face blurs when he leans closer to my face. His warm lips skim my cheek, and damn, it fills my heart with so much love, I fear it's going to implode any second.

"I want the man I know would never let me go and who will hold me through all my darkest nights. I want a crazy man who can be my best friend and watch *All the Bright Places* a hundred times just because it has my name in it."

He moves to my jaw, nipping lightly, helping me shrug out of my shirt. I place my palm on his chest, feeling the wild thudding of his heart as he gazes into my eyes.

"I want to own the back seat of your bike for this life and kiss you under the spitting sky. Not just friendly pecks on the lips, but how you kissed me now, full of passion and desire. I want you to serve my sweet tooth until we're too old and all my teeth have fallen off. I want the man I know I can't live a day without because if I did, I would be fucking miserable, Adri."

He groans when I pull back to admire the love shining in his eyes. It's so potent and mesmerizing that I can't move or breathe. I don't realize how my emotions run down in silent resignation until he draws a finger down the side of my cheek and wipes away the wet trail there.

"I'm in love with you, Violet, and nothing feels as perfect as you in my arms. You're my home." Adrian murmurs. I can't stand the space between us any longer and band my arms around him, hanging on for my dear life. His breath is hot against my neck and my lips as he chants my name, whispers his love for me, and I feel it with every beat of my heart.

It's my love song.

24 | You're My Waltz

They say when you fall in love, you don't have a choice but to let your guard down. I did the same with Adrian. I pushed my insecurities aside and entered the love castle he created for us, bare feet. And God, did he let me reign his heart like a queen?

When I woke up this morning, my cheek pressed against his gloriously naked back - I realized it wasn't all a dream. He had come back to me. Our separation was over, and we were finally ready to start our story from the very beginning.

I lay on my back and press a hand against my chest, blinking against the morning sun. Last night was the night of reunion and naked truths. And this morning is all about reminiscing the beautiful marks he left on my heart and body.

Shifting toward the man responsible for my newfound passion and desires, I place a smile against the curve of his bicep. He groans something unintelligible in his sleep, throwing his hand over my waist and pulling me against his side.

Face down in my bed, hugging me like his favorite teddy bear, and the permanent, gentle scowl makes me bite a smile tugging on my lips. I admire his thick dark lashes fanning toward sharp cheekbones and the purple bite mark I left across his jaw. If there's one thing I wanted the most, it would be waking up wrapped in his warmth every morning.

He shifts, kissing the top of my head in his sleep. Sweet lord in heaven, he is deliciously nude, the line of his spine cutting a groove between toned shoulders and a slim waist. Adrian surely outruns me in having a fit body and a purposeful mind.

When he's on his back, I feather my fingers over the flower of my name tattooed over his heart, follow the dips of his abs but stop myself from disturbing his sleep. It is six in the morning, and we slept only a couple of hours ago, thanks to our long-due need for each other.

His breath stumbles at my touch, and he cracks open his eyes to regard me with his half-mast gaze.

"You're awake, V?" He rasps groggily, creeping a hand toward my face, sliding away the strand of hair from my bare shoulder, and planting a hot kiss on my collarbone.

"Good morning to you too, Adri," I smile, trailing kisses over his shoulder.

He leans over and kisses me lazily on the corner of my mouth, making me want to pounce him. I wrap my legs around his waist and seek out a kiss on my lips.

"Hey now," he says softly, biting his lower lip and eyes fixed on my mouth. "I have to be somewhere important this morning. And if we kiss now, I'm afraid I won't be able to make it on time."

"I don't care." The words come out a little breathless. "I've just got you after months. Everything else can wait."

He looks down at my face from where he's leaning above me, his palms planted on the bed, either side of my head, flashing one of his playful smiles. "How are you so perfect for me, little sinner?"

I never thought I would be blushing and breaking eye contact with a boy whom I had known since I was thirteen, but right this moment, as his heated gaze caresses my face, I flush evenly. "You're right. You should go before dad finds out you jumped through my window again last night."

"Shh," he places a finger on my lips, then trails it down to my throat, tracing circles over my sternum. His breath comes out in a ragged exhale that turns into a curse. "I thought about it all the time...kissing you on your mouth."

I blink a few times, gulping away the anticipation that formed in my throat. Just like that, his mood changes from casual to passionate in a second, and it doesn't fail to entice me every single time.

"Morning breath, Adri. Let's brush our teeth and -" he kisses the words from my mouth with a passion that has both urgency and peace. He bends over me, framing my face with his elbows, his hands lacing through my hair. With every growing second, it gets intense, his determined and starved mouth making love with mine. He kisses me deeply, with barely suppressed ferocity, and I feel myself melting against him.

Then he leaves me high on his kiss, pulling away in a flash. By the time I recover from the ecstasy and rise on my elbows to look over him, he's already stepping out of my window. He's dressed only in briefs, his clothes thrown carelessly over his shoulder.

"Adri, that's not fair. Come back!" I shout breathlessly, holding the sheets to my chest.

"I'll come for you in the evening, love." He winks at me with a smug grin, leaning on my window ledge. "But I've got to go now."

***

This place is familiar - our high school. So many of our teenage memories remain infused inside these brick walls. Some beautiful, others not so much, but none easy to forget. However, what takes me by surprise though, is the decoration. It looks exactly how I saw in pictures all those years back, the prom I missed.

Adrian stands in front of me, dressed in a tailored black tuxedo, his hair a messy arrangement atop his head and his sweet, endearing smile glowing across his face.

It must have taken him an entire day to decorate the gymnasium, turning it into a high school prom, and he didn't miss a trick.

"Do you like it, V?" He asks, picking one of the heart-shaped balloons around my feet and offering it to me with a grin. "I wanted to take you to the prom, and now that I finally have the courage, I want to do this perfectly."

I chuckle, taking the balloon from his hand. "This is perfect. Everything is just as I had imagined. You, me, us, and this."

He pulls me to himself in a quick move, his hands sliding around my waist and his minty breath fanning over my face. His expression shows the raw affection in his voice as he caresses my jaw with his thumb and stares at my mouth. "You look like a dream in this violet dress, my little sinner. I wish we didn't miss that prom in our junior year. I'm sure I would've done this much, much earlier."

"What-"

He leaves me hanging on that one word as he closes the gap between our mouths and kisses me. His tall frame envelopes me, vibrating with pure certainty and power. His hands tangle in my hair, and his mouth devours my gasp as I claw the balloon he gave me, busting it. We don't break from the kiss, tasting and savoring each other's needs.

Despite the urgency surrounding us, his mouth is gentle against mine. A tender kiss is what we share. He licks across the inside of my upper lip, then nips the bottom one. "I never want to stop doing this," he whispers against my lips.

"Then we won't," I confirm, tracing the sharp line of his jaw, practically humming with the thought that this beautiful man is all mine to keep.

"I thought I had lost you forever, V." He lifts my hand and touches his lips against the inside of my wrist. "You've no idea the hell I went through to let you choose Augustus over me, knowing that it was all my fault in the first place."

Your name, *Dear Augustus*, hardens my stomach. Even after a year, my heart caves whenever I remember your amber eyes and golden hair resembling the sunshine you reflect through your dimpled smile. I feel the loss all over again. But as always, I'm pulled to the shore with two arresting green eyes. And there's peace and solidarity in the way he holds me together, not letting me break, now, ever.

With a shiver, I shake my head, roaming my hands across his shirt and tracing the rigid muscle beneath. "No, none of this is your fault or mine. We were young and reckless and maybe a little naïve too."

He nods, eyes hard and unblinking as he takes a step away and holds out his hand for me. "Violet Eve, can I have this dance with you? I promise to behave and keep my hands to myself as much as possible."

"Yes," I laugh, taking his hand and letting him guide me to the middle of the room. He pulls out his phone and plays *Until I Found You* by Stephen Sanchez as we sway to the music, my hands on his shoulders, his around my waist. Then we are closer, chest to chest, hand in hand, hearts beating.

I place my head over his heart and listen to my favorite music, his heartbeat. And this is the song I can always listen to on repeat.

"I can never have enough of you." He yanks me closer, his breath at my ear, making me shudder.

"Not very successful in keeping your hands to yourself, are you Mr. Adrian Hayes?" I kiss his neck and whisper in his ear.

He moves his hands up my sides and holds my cheeks in his palms, making me look into his ocean eyes. "I've been waiting to take you on this date for so long, and now that we're finally here, all I want is this evening to end so I can take you to my bed and do everything else that's on my mind."

"What's in your mind, Adri?" My lungs pant with excitement.

"You, just you," he bends closer and strokes his thumb across my throat, his touch possessive and comforting. At my shuddering sigh, he brushes a lock of my hair behind my ear. "To have you in every way possible, tonight and forever."

And he does have me, forever.

The End

Epilogue | Augustus

I let her go twice, and both times it broke my heart.

And she is no more my familiar stranger. She is just a stranger. Now that I have lost her, I realize what a fool I was to let her go. It tears my heart that she's no more my destiny. I keep my eyes closed, holding the pain inside, strumming the familiar tune as every moment spent with her reels inside my mind.

I am not the only traveler

Who has not repaid his debt

I've been searching for a trail to follow again

Take me back to the night we met...

I'm sitting on a bench in Central Park, busking, wearing a mask and goggles, dressed in an overcoat to cover up my tats and any resemblance to my present reputation. Being a known face has its downside. You can't just sit in a park and play songs on a Sunday morning. But right now, as I sit with my old guitar, my case sitting on the ground with a few bucks shining against the black velvet, I'm not the infamous *August* Z. I'm just Augustus.

Every once in a while, I try to reconnect with my old self, no matter how broken it is. And every time, with the same hope that I can move on from the girl named Violet, my first love. I don't know how to stop hurting. So, I let the pain flow out of my soul and into the guitar, voicing it through my words.

And then I can tell myself

What the hell I'm supposed to do

And then I can tell myself

Not to ride along with you...

I look up and find myself staring at the young couple gathered with the crowd around me. The guy with blue eyes bends down and gives a butterfly kiss to the girl holding an ice cream in her hand. A smile tugs at my lips with the memories of her. I remember all the feathery touches we shared, the gentle kisses we stole, and the comfort of holding her close to my heart.

I had all and then most of you

Some and now none of you

Take me back to the night we met

I don't know what I'm supposed to do

Haunted by the ghost of you

Oh, take me back to the night we met...

We were bound to fall apart. I knew it the day she chose me, even though her heart wasn't there when she was with me. I saw it when Adrian walked away from her. She wasn't my Violet anymore. She had moved on. Even then, I wished my love would be enough for both of us, but that's not how you fight for someone you love. When you love someone, you need them to be equally invested in the relationship.

So, I had to let her go for good this time, with no promises, no hope that we'll meet again, a forever goodbye.

My fingers falter on the strings, a wave of heartache seeping into my ribcage and leaving me struggling to move into the next verse. Then I hear you, my familiar stranger. You emerge from the crowd with an acoustic guitar in your hand and a smile that whispers promises of a new connection. Your voice, laced in honey, and wrapped in silk, continues my song as I meet your gaze, strumming the tune.

When the night was full of terrors
And your eyes were filled with tears
When you had not touched me yet
Oh, take me back to the night we met...

You don't stop among the crowd. Instead, head straight towards my bench and sit at the other end. As your maple-colored hair falls on your face, my fingers twitch to brush them aside.

I don't miss how your pale ivory skin glows under the sun. You bite your lip with my attention. Your eyes never leave mine as you adjust the guitar on your lap, fingers on the fretboard, and then you join in my tune. Perfect sync. You don't know my name, I've never asked yours, but we meet every Sunday, same time, in this place and with a new song.

I laugh softly, shaking my head as you nudge your chin with that captivating smirk at the group of teenage girls huddled around our bench. And we begin the final verse together, drawing the attention of anyone who seems to hear us.

I had all and then most of you
Some and now none of you
Take me back to the night we met
I don't know what I'm supposed to do
Haunted by the ghost of you
Take me back to the night we met...

I sing it to the haunting and sad memories of lost love. When you sing it, you smother it with new possibilities and hope. Maybe one day, when my heart stops aching, I can write you a song, and we can sing it as a duet.

Not today.

My heart is yet to heal, but it has almost found its cure.

Almost.

Take me back to the night we met...

Author's Note

There are so many kinds of love, each as magical as the other. Sometimes, growing is letting go, and that may leave a gaping hole in your heart. But new love always finds its way to make your heart whole again.

For Violet and Augustus, heartbreak was inevitable. I do believe that you are capable of loving two people. However, you can't love them in the same timeline. So, I want you to embrace this harsh truth with an open heart.

Dear Augustus has finally ended, and I'm still trying to work around that fact. I'm so happy that you loved and supported me through this journey.

Recommend Dear Augustus to your friends and leave a review if it touched your heart.

Thanks for reading!

xoxo,

Pooja

Playlist

"Another Love" - Tom Odell

"Atlantis" - Seafret

"Snap" - Rosa Linn

"Let It Be Me" - Ray LaMontagne

"Long Gone and Moved On" - The Script

"The Night We Met" - Lord Huron

"Summertime Sadness" - Lana Del Rey

"Falling" - Harry Styles

"Let Her Go" - Passenger

"Heartburn" - Wafia

"Hurts So Good" - Astrid S

"Call You Mine" - The Chainsmokers

"Send My Love" - Adele

"In the Name of Love" - Bebe Rexha and Martin Garrix

"Say You Won't Let Go" - James Arthur

"I Won't Give Up" - Jason Mraz

"Until I Found You" - Stephen Sanchez

Acknowledgements

Ma, Papa, and my siblings thank you for your tireless love and support. You really are my heroes. Our battles with a brain tumor have changed how I perceived things earlier. We proved - we can move mountains when we are together. The bravery we projected and the positivity we reflected toward something so critical made me realize how I can do better by simply living my life to the fullest. No regrets. No complaints. Although I wrote this book way before we got diagnosed with the critical illness, I had to keep it on hold. The last few months have been incredibly tough and emotionally draining, but we stood strong in the face of our demons and came out as scarred knights. I love you so much! Thank you for being the best family ever.

It feels bitter-sweet to wrap up this two-part novella series. Dear Augustus, was my first attempt at an emotional romance and can very well be considered the basis of my later works. It's overwhelming to mark it as complete and move on, but I'm so relieved at the same time.

Even though I've advanced toward writing adult fiction, this series will forever remain my favorite. The reason is my unfiltered emotions that went into these characters and how they bleed perfectly through my words. I wanted to write something simple yet edgy. I wanted to write something sweet but sad and hard to forget.

In January 2022, I signed the first installment of the series with my publisher, and it almost took me a year for the second one. Thank you to the entire team at Author's Ink Publications, who worked hard to present my story in the most amazing form.

Thank you to my beta readers, Kristina Ghukasyan and Shreya Shrikumar. Your suggestions made this story so much better. Thanks to Divesh Agarwal and Kaushiki Bose, my fellow author friends, for being my dedicated readers and motivating me to complete the series.

Thanks to my friends and teammates who are there for me, whether it is about publishing, overthinking, or life in general.

And finally, my wonderful readers, thanks for loving and praising my first novella, *Dear Augustus Before I Let Go;* you made me write this second book.

About The Author

Pooja Pathak is a passionate storyteller with a knack for creating complex yet realistic characters. Her debut novella '*Dear Augustus, Before I Let Go*' published in 2021, gained a lot of praise from readers for its literary style and raw storytelling. She has also written non-fiction books -*Ashes to Embers* and *Little Things Matter*, poetry, and prose on self-help and healing. Currently, she lives in Mumbai, Maharashtra. When she's not working on a business scenario and creating dashboards, she can be found at her desk, writing emotional romances. *Dear Augustus, I Never Let Go* is the second book in the *Dear Augustus* novella series.

Connect with her at...

Instagram: https://www.instagram.com/pooja.silentwordz/

Twitter: https://twitter.com/_poojapathak

Email: pathak.pooja8894@gmail.com

Also by Pooja Pathak

Dear Augustus, Before I Let Go
Ashes to Embers
Little Things Matter

www.ingramcontent.com/pod-product-compliance
Lightning Source LLC
LaVergne TN
LVHW091454170726
843492LV00001B/177